"Jax Cassidy is delightful! Her lush, lyrical way with words will draw you in and keep you turning the pages."
— Sylvia Day, National Bestselling Author

"Jax Cassidy serves up great sex with emotional intensity--what more can a reader want?"
— Kayla Perrin, Author of GETTING EVEN and OBSESSION

"[Siren's Seduction...] A delicious tale of love and lust, and two lost souls who find each other—I loved it."
— Sunny, National Bestselling Author

"Fluid, lyrical and with a unique sensitivity to her characters, Jax Cassidy's work is as sensual as it is emotional. This is definitely an author to keep your eye on!"
— Eden Bradley, Author of FORBIDDEN FRUIT

"Jax Cassidy is a brilliant new voice in contemporary fiction. Full of heat, seduction, and romance, her winning characters are sure to capture your heart and find a place on your keeper shelf."
— Gemma Halliday, Author of the
SPYING IN HIGH HEELS series

Art of Sensuality

A Novel By

JAX CASSIDY

BOOK LIST

The Lotus Blossom Chronicles, Book One
SIREN'S SEDUCTION

The Lotus Blossom Chronicles, Book Four
LOVE'S HEALING GARDEN

CASSIDY KENT

Published through Amber Quill Press
One Wicked Winter
Santa's Helper
Dear John
What Lies in Winter

Published through Phaze Publishing
Fortune's Fool
Sunset Key
Raleigh in Rio
Dolce & Diana
Miranda Writes
Sonnet Seduction

Art of Sensuality

A Novel By

JAX CASSIDY

Dedication

For Ted.
Thank you for lighting the passions
and stoking the fires of creativity.
Chivalry is not lost.
Je t'aime.

Acknowledgements

First off, thank you Parker. You are missed.

This has been an amazing journey for me as a writer and as an individual. I wouldn't be here today without the wonderful people who have shaped my life.

For my parents, thank you for giving me so much and loving me unconditionally.

To Jessalyn and Kyme, thank you for being the best sisters a girl could ever have!

To Kristen Painter, you're fabulous! I aspire to be like you! Thank you for believing in me from the get-go.

To Eden Bradley, my surrogate sister, thank you for sharing in on the fun times, as well as supporting me during the difficult ones. You've inspired me with your hard work and perseverance.

To Eva Gale, I couldn't survive without our daily chats, your humor and infinite wisdom. Your friendship, love, and encouragement have touched my jaded heart.

To Gemma Halliday, thanks for your pep talks, juicy gossip on dating, and sharing in on life's struggles and successes.

To Lara Santiago, I admire your prolific writing skills and fun-loving spirit! Thanks for allowing me into your secret "girls club".

To Lillian Feisty, R.G. Alexander, and Crystal Jordan, thanks for being there for the laughter, cheers, and tears.

To Night Diva Maria, thank you for loving my stories. You're the best! I can't say it enough.

To Jesse, you are my best guy pal. Thank you for the brainstorming sessions and driving cross-country with me. I can't imagine riding this roller coaster without you.

To Anne Aaronson, thanks for journeying with me outside of the writing realm.

To my G-crew, Denita, Mimi, Brandy, Julie, and Jennifer, love you all and miss you a bunch!

To the Romance Divas and Dudes for your love!

Finally, to my wonderful Parker Publishing family: Miriam, Jackie, Miriam Jr., Jeff, Erin, Kymberlyn, Tony & Lucinda. You make me proud to be a part of the team. I love you all!

Chapter One

O cean waves flowed inland like silken sheets, rolling across the soft stretch of sand. The water spread upwards, spraying specks of liquid on Caleb Holden's tennis shoes and jogging pants. The chilly morning air caressed his face and bare arms as he continued his steady morning run across the beach.

Caleb slowed his pace as he neared the routine end point, two houses from his own. He stopped at the edge of the familiar glass house to catch his breath, his heart pumping hard against his chest as he bent forward, hands on hips, to inhale a lungful of air.

This morning he had run harder than he had in quite a while and it felt good to push his body beyond the limit. He experienced a sense of accomplishment every time his calf muscles throbbed in pain. *No pain, no gain.* The clichéd motto was a theme that often ran through his mind in regards to everything in his life. He believed pain was just a reminder of his mortality and the necessary force to reach his goals. Success was all the sweeter when he tasted the sweat of his labors.

Caleb took a few deep breaths. Leveling out, he straightened up to go. Out of the corner of his eye he caught a glimpse of dim lights flickering from inside his neighbor's home. *Who could be up at 3:45 AM?*

"Strange. They must be back early this year," he whispered under his breath. Curiosity got the best of him and Caleb looked through the oversized window of the massive modern construction composed of glass, concrete and steel. The Delacroix's home was a breathtakingly elegant and slick design worthy of any magazine feature. A graceful masterpiece he had wanted to purchase but accepted the offer a few days short.

Caleb had fallen in love immediately with the architecture for its clean, yet tranquil, Zen appeal. "Sustainable design" was what Luc Delacroix had proudly emphasized years ago when he had asked about the unique appearance. From what he understood, this was a response to the global environmental crisis and would contribute to the environment by reducing use of non-renewable resources. He thought it would bring people back to their natural environment by being "green".

Of course, Caleb had a newfound respect for his neighbor after that education. He was quick to install solar panels in his home and did some eco-friendly landscaping on his modest yard. One thing was certain; Luc was a man ahead of his time. Since then, the neighbors who had once ridiculed Luc for being a "tree hugger" were now following suite in droves. All in the name of tax breaks, not for the environmental cause.

Caleb made a mental note to stop in later to greet his seasonal neighbors. He always enjoyed Luc's lively conversations and open-mindedness towards diverse topics from art to the stock market. They had shared many dinner parties and drunken dialogues in which their bond only grew stronger with time. This was a huge change from his introverted, unfriendly neighbors and if not for Luc, living in Manhattan Beach wouldn't be nearly as bearable, or as entertaining.

He smiled to himself in remembrance of their last get together. His breath caught in his throat when he took a quick glance inside. Alarm bells went off in his head and he stepped in closer for another look. He had known the Delacroix to have house guests every so often, so he didn't believe she was any kind of burglar. She certainly didn't look like one either.

Who was she?

He would have remembered meeting her if they had been introduced. Caleb decided it would be best to call Luc when he got back to his home. He didn't want to jump to any conclusions without sorting it out with them first. He had intended to leave, yet being a hot-blooded male; he opted for a closer look at the Delacroix's houseguest.

How was she connected to the Delacroix?

He looked around, hoping the neighbors wouldn't catch him and get the wrong idea. Maybe he was acting a little paranoid, but he felt like a voyeur viewing the most intimate and private moments of a stranger. Her profile revealed a striking beauty, an exotic goddess bathed in candlelight.

Everything about her appearance seemed delicate and innocent, yet strong at the same time. His eyes skimmed across her face, her slender yet seductive body, to her curved hips that were accentuated in the short cutoffs. Her long midnight-black hair flowed across her back, spilling across her arms, and adding to her sensual allure.

The woman was petite in stature but her toned arms and legs hinted at a quiet strength, perhaps maintained from a rigid exercise routine like yoga or Pilates. Her youthful features and silky skin were enhanced by almond-shaped eyes with thick dark lashes, a button nose and high cheekbones. What drew him most to her exotic Amerasian features were those naturally rosy lips, so plump and perfect. Lush lips that were made to be kissed, worshipped, and devoured with slow subtlety.

Caleb blinked as if she was an illusion caused by his strenuous run. Yet there she was, kneeling on the floor, staring up at an oversized canvas. One moment she appeared to be in control of her emotions and the next she doubled over, her body shaking as she wept. The tears flowed on and her sorrow painted an image he would most likely never forget.

How could a total stranger affect him this way? His stomach tightened with a natural desire to console her, hold her in his arms and discover what caused her such pain. This reaction was so foreign and as bizarre as it seemed, he could almost believe the Universe was pulling him toward her.

Caleb inched in closer. He noticed the splatters of paint across her golden skin and clothes. She gripped a paintbrush in her hand. Fresh paint still glistening on its tip. She appeared as graceful as her own painting and his body tingled with an unfamiliar sensation. The paints called to him and he longed to touch the wet paint, then trail his fingers across her flawless skin. Wanted to spread the colors around as if she was an unfinished masterpiece that only he could complete.

Get a grip, Holden. What the hell am I doing?

He blinked, as if that action would break the spell. Somehow his fascination wouldn't allow him to look away and his eyes kept returning to *her*. God, she was simply exquisite. A delicate beauty that resembled the woman on the canvas itself, yet the image had a subtle eroticism that surrounded the innocent face. Naked flesh revealed through a sheer flowing crimson gown, posed seductively, almost as if the painting embodied a message he wanted to decipher.

Leave it to him to rationalize everything with a psychological analysis. His eyes caught sight of other canvases from the flicker of candles she used as a light source. Caleb squinted for a better look, his eyes skimming across the room. Several life-sized paintings were propped along the wall and against the various furniture.

He didn't know what to make of the discovery. All the women had identical faces except for their hairstyles and color, the same sensuality reflecting in their eyes, their lips. If he stared hard enough he would believe they could come to life and weave their magic over him. He swallowed hard. The paintings made him as breathless as the artist who painted them.

As if she sensed him watching, she lifted her head to stare out the window. Straight at him. Caleb reacted without thought, quickly stepping backwards in hopes that he could escape detection. Guilt washed over him for peeping at her grief-filled moment. A right he did not have. Without acting like his usual sensible self, he did the one thing he hadn't done since a teenager.

Caleb ran like hell back to his home.

๑๛๑

Machiko wiped her eyes across her forearm. Crying hadn't helped alleviate the deep sorrow lingering in her soul. She felt the emptiness even after years spent trying to overcome the emotion. Years of psychologists, psychiatrists and treatment to 'undo' her withdrawal from the outside world. How could she explain to others what led to her breakdown at thirteen or her estrangement from her parents at sixteen?

After time she learned to accept her idiosyncrasies and ignored the people who had called her a loner. Eccentric. She didn't care about the labels society placed upon her and focused on ways to heal herself without the team of doctors hovering over her. By sheer luck she had landed a job as an au pair when her roommate begged her to go in her place when she could not cancel the assignment at the last minute.

Briana had vouched for her and the rest was up to Machiko to re-invent herself. She could finally start over in a foreign country and fit into a strange new place where there were no preconceived notions. A place where she could be accepted for all her eccentricities without fear of having her identity uncovered.

She was finally free. So why did she still feel the emotional incarceration deep in her gut? Would she ever fill the gap of continual yearning, find the missing pieces to the jigsaw puzzle that plagued her daily? She knew this unfulfilled part of her had been from swearing off her love of painting, until now. Then how could she explain the emptiness that lingered inside even though she had broken her vow to never paint again?

Anger surged through her and Machiko got up from her pathetic position on the hardwood floor. She couldn't believe she had stayed in the house for two whole weeks without giving into temptation until today. Machiko couldn't escape the madness that overcame her and she had finally given in. She had torn through the art supplies like a starved man at a buffet.

She blamed it on the madness, the transformation that had been planted in her head like a seed that slowly blossomed. Luc Delacroix's words echoed through her head. *Don't waste your talents. Don't deprive art lovers by hiding the beauty which you are able to create. You were meant for this. You were born to paint.*

The Delacroix had thought they were so clever to propose she housesit for them when she knew damn well they had a deep desire for her to produce pieces for their gallery. Charlotte was a kind woman and very poor at fabricating stories. Over the nine years of service as au pair, Machiko had learned to read the woman and decipher the truths behind her words.

The images of two strikingly beautiful children with disheveled blonde hair and mischievous twinkles in their eyes came to her mind. She smiled at the thought of little Didier and Genevieve who had managed to keep her art teachings a secret from their parents for the past two years. It wasn't until Luc Delacroix had discovered the stash of artworks hidden in the children's closet and brought it to her attention that the cat was out of the bag.

Machiko bent down to gather the used paint brushes and walked over to the studio sink. She rinsed out the paints from the brushes before laying them flat across the towel on the counter. She caught a glimpse of her stained hands and arms and it comforted her. The paints felt like a sturdy armor secured around her, protecting her from the harsh, demanding, lonely world.

She did not know how she could deny herself the only pleasures she had ever known for so long. Her stomach squeezed and the searing pain returned. She knew very well why. Machiko had single handedly destroyed her parents' credibility and reputation with a single lie. Not a day passed without a painful reminder of this fact and the guilt she carried with her all these years became the burdens that sat on her shoulders, in her conscience.

The room seemed constricting and Machiko suddenly

needed air. She walked barefoot through the house and stepped out onto the porch that overlooked the ocean. She leaned her stomach against the wooden railing and closed her eyes, inhaling deeply of the cool, salty air. Energy flowed through her body, relaxing her to the core while the soft breeze caressed her face and made her aware of the peacefulness of the early morning.

A yawn escaped her and weariness took over. Had she been awake for almost twenty-four hours now? Painting tended to make her forget time and place. The act was a drug she didn't want to kick. Her stomach growled and she ignored the sound. She would eat later, but first she would take a hot shower and hope that when she slept the recurring dreams would not take root again.

✸

The stranger stroked her face, his hands sliding down her arms, across her ribcage before he gripped her buttocks in his strong hands. She arched her back and felt his lips gently grazing her neck. She turned her head so he could have easier access and he flicked his tongue across her flesh. Her body trembled in anticipation, making her ache to be taken. Violated, worshipped, fulfilled.

He leaned his body in closer, pressing himself between her thighs and the stirrings of desire inched its way through her. She raised her hips, desperate to feel the closeness and he groaned against her throat. The stranger reached up and grabbed a fistful of her hair, pulling her head back before he captured her lips. His kiss was hard, demanding, and greedy as he explored her mouth.

She reached around him and dug her nails into his back. He growled, deepening the kiss, his tongue dueling with hers with the same eagerness and frantic passion. She felt his rock-hard shaft against her stomach, which only increased her cravings. She captured his tongue, sucking gently and the simple act had pleased him. He lifted her ass to position her and in one swift motion he entered her, answering her pleas, filling her up in more ways than one.

He moved slowly at first until she understood the rhythm, until she matched his. His movements increased as he slid in and out of her with long, smooth strokes. His kisses growing intense as they moved together, dancing to a song only their hearts could hear. She urged him on with her hips, her mouth, her hands. Their bodies spoke in a secret language as he pumped into her, hard and fast. Her moans escalated until her senses roared to life and the slow buildup became a tight energy ball that needed to detonate.

Her body heated up, consumed by a fire that stirred within like the vibrant colors of her paints when she mixed them together. They created a complete composition, well balanced, a cohesive structure and color scheme. The faster he moved the wetter she became until the pressure was too much for her. She could feel the tension coiling tighter, his body taking control, leaving her helpless and without strength to fight the inevitable.

Do you really want to fight it?

A strange repetitive shrill broke through her senses and Machiko jolted awake. Her heart hammering in her chest, her body tense, her sex screaming out its disappointment.

She let out a hollow sigh and reached for the phone on her nightstand.

Disappointment was an emotion she knew all too well.

❦

"Fuck. Fuck. Double fuck!" Machiko yelled as she ran through the house toward the kitchen. Smoke billowed from the oven and she yanked open the metal door. The quick drop made it bounce on its hinges. The sounds of the fire detector going off was deafening to the ears. She took one look at the metal cookie sheet and the charred remains of her once perfect balls of dough laughed back at her.

Machiko grabbed a baking mitt and shoved her hand through it before pulling out the tray, kicking the door shut with her foot. She dropped the cookie sheet on the stove, threw off the mitt, and started opening all the glass doors and windows she could get to before she dealt with the alarm.

A loud banging on her front door added to her annoyance and she ignored the sound. When the pounding didn't stop and the shrill of the alarm grated heavily on her nerves she ran to the door and opened it without looking through the peephole. "What?"

"Well, hello…" the man began, his brows drew together and without finishing his greeting he stepped around her and went straight for the source of the irritating noise. The stranger reached up and pulled the lid off the smoke detector before pulling out the battery to silence the device.

"Fuckin' annoying things," he muttered to no one in particular before turning to meet her gaze. She had managed to follow him and realized it had been an error in judgment.

Machiko stood inches from him and when she had fully focused in on his face her chest tightened oddly, her body temperature rising. *My God, he was perfect*. Her heart stopped.

The man had remarkable features. Piercing toffee eyes with a gentleness to them, high cheekbones, a strong, square jaw. To top it off, his thick mass of spiky dark hair only accentuated his sexy, rugged good looks. He reminded her of a sleek athlete mixed with a catalog model appeal like a David Beckham or a Tom Brady. Not so bulky, just lean and masculine.

"Welcome to the neighborhood," he announced in a rich voice that made her knees suddenly grow wobbly. The man shoved a covered dish at her and all she could do was stare. She didn't know how long she had paused; her eyes were glued to those lips, that wide grin which slowly dissolved into a frown.

"This is the part where you take the gift and thank me," he instructed in a tone that made her feel like a child that couldn't grasp simple instructions.

"Um, thanks." She felt like an idiot and grabbed the dish from him. "What is it? And who are you?"

"Cookies. From the smell of things, it looks like you aren't a seasoned baker. Better leave it to the pros."

Machiko didn't know what to make of the man. He had a take-charge demeanor. Had managed to dismantle her alarm like a hero rescuing a damsel in distress, yet when he opened his mouth he had practically insulted her twice in two sentences.

"Excuse me?" She emphasized with attitude.

"No offense, but I'm afraid the burnt cookie smell may take a while to air out." He winked as if he were trying to turn up the charm.

Somehow his action made her defensive and she couldn't wait to get rid of him fast enough.

"Thanks for the gift but now I've got a lot of cleanup work to do." She turned abruptly and headed for the front door, which was still wide open from moments ago. She didn't hear the footsteps behind her and whirled around to see if he was going to follow.

His expression, the strength of his stance, the intense glint in his eyes made her think of a Gladiator preparing for battle. *Look away*. Why did he make her feel so unhinged? Nervous, anxious, uncomfortable, yet so aroused.

Her body hummed. There was definitely a strange pull of attraction so strong she needed to look away before she made a fool of herself. She would most likely gawk at him as if she'd never seen a man before. Her skills in the social conversation department had always been lacking and someone who looked like *him* never glanced her way, let alone wanted to engage in conversation with her.

"Are you always this friendly?"

He started to move toward her and she took a step back. The man frowned at her response, then his expression changed. He appeared to relax, showing her a flash of white teeth as he smiled at her. "Hey, I can see I caught you at a bad time. I'm one of your neighbors, two houses down. Come by anytime if you need anything." He headed for the door and stopped right at the frame. "I work from home so don't hesitate to drop by. I'm sure you'd need a cup of sugar or a bottle of wine sometime when you aren't in the mood to run to the nearest store. I've got plenty in stock."

His words came out in one long stream and she couldn't help biting back a smile. His actions were almost boyish and he seemed like a man who craved company. She, however, was the complete opposite and relished the solitude. Loved shutting herself off from society if she had a choice.

"Thanks. I'm sure I won't be needing anything." She attempted a smile, a little out of practice, and hoped she had at least sounded friendlier. *Just go already.* If he stuck around any longer she was ready to shove him out the door.

As if a light bulb clicked in her head, an old memory resurfaced. She recalled the first time her body reacted this way and her stomach knotted at the thought.

Lust.

He nodded in understanding but his eyes seemed to be sending her a message she couldn't read. Those beautiful chocolate eyes she could drown in if she wasn't careful.

"If you change your mind…" he let the sentence hang and turned to leave without waiting for her response.

She watched him continue down the steps and along the sandy path. When he disappeared in the distance, she finally let out her breath.

The knot tightened.

All signs pointed to trouble. He was a six-foot, hunky temptation just two doors down and the kind that oozed a whole mess of trouble she shouldn't entertain the thought of getting to know.

Chapter Two

Machiko dug her feet deeper into the sand. She always loved the mix of powdery and grainy textures as it wrapped around her skin. She loved the salty smell that blew in from the wind. Loved the sound of the ocean waves that was a pure slice of heaven to her mind, body, senses. So tranquil and inspiring.

She hugged her legs closer to her chest and closed her eyes, leaning her head on her knees. The sun warmed her back and she couldn't have asked for a more perfect day. The peacefulness of the morning, accompanied with the lullaby of the water, made her want to drift off into far off lands created in her mind's eye. Machiko could almost taste paradise.

"You there," a musical voice interrupted her serene moment.

She opened her eyes, turning her head toward the house next door. An older woman stood on the porch, waving happily to garner her attention. The bright red, orange, and green colors and abstract designs of the woman's robe assaulted her eyes, and instantly she knew they were destined to be kindred souls.

Machiko sat up and waved in acknowledgement. "Good morning."

"Would you like some tea?" The woman asked in a pleasant, watered-down accent, perhaps a fusion of British and American.

"Sounds great." Machiko kicked off the sand and stood up, brushing the remnants of the powdery specks off her clothes. She took her time walking, simply concentrating on the feel of the sand tickling her feet. She reached the cozy, cottage-style house and the warmth and vibrancy of the place seemed to welcome her. Very bohemian-chic, very much like the woman who inhabited it.

She took the wooden steps up and walked through the open porch gate. Why did she accept the invitation? She wasn't one to gravitate to anyone, but her curiosity overcame her need to be alone today. She missed the Delacroix children and company didn't sound too bad.

Machiko had her first glimpse of her colorful neighbor. Up close, the woman was a bombshell. She could have easily been mistaken for Raquel Welch, the sex symbol of the swinging 60s and early 70s. The woman's classic beauty and elegance was downplayed by the loud attire and spunky demeanor.

"You new around here?" The woman eyed her.

"Just housesitting."

"You must be somethin' real special. How'd you manage that gig?" She smiled, offering her hand. "Francesca Lincoln. But you can call me Frankie."

"Machiko, the au pair. Have been for about nine years now." She shook Frankie's hand.

"Just Machiko?" Frankie sounded amused.

Her answer firm. "Just Machiko."

"Well, why don't you take a seat at the table over there and I'll be back in a flash with some tea." Frankie walked off in the direction of the French doors leading into the house.

Machiko made her way to the café-style table with a contemporary metal frame. She sat down on the matching chair with its bright, yet tasteful embroidered, floral patterned cushion.

This house appeared simplistic but every detail proved to be precise, well thought out and decorated. She looked down at the tabletop; the jewel-encrusted, intricate floral work caught her attention. *Simply amazing.* The person who designed it was a true artist. She could not imagine the time and patience it must have taken to strategically place every dime-sized jewel with such expertise to create a shading effect.

She traced her fingers around the jewels, marveling in the flow of the pattern. She became so absorbed that she didn't hear Frankie return.

"I can tell you have an appreciation for art." Frankie placed a tray of tea and pastries on the table.

Machiko looked up, grinning. "It's incredible. You must have paid a pretty penny for it."

"Well, it would have cost more if I hadn't been the one doing the design. It was a bitch to get everything the way I wanted it though."

"You did this? Somehow I'm not surprised."

Frankie poured the hot liquid into the teacups and handed one to Machiko. "Take a pastry and tell me about yourself, Mac."

Mac? She normally hated nicknames but coming from Frankie it was a compliment, sounded natural. This was something the woman possibly only reserved for people she liked. The thought made her smile inside.

"Funny that the Delacroix never brought you back with them all these years." Frankie took a hearty bite of a cheese Danish.

Machiko reached out and grabbed a butter croissant. "Actually, I chose not to go. I'd housesit for them in Paris while they came here. This way, they could spend time as a family without needing a nanny to watch the kids." Machiko pulled off an end and popped it into her mouth.

Frankie polished off her Danish and picked up the creamer, pouring some into her cup. "Care for some?"

She nodded. "Tea just isn't the same without a spot of cream."

"I know what you mean. Living overseas seeps into your soul. The traditions soon become your own."

Frankie chirped happily, "That it does. I like to visit my lovely countryside of Rotherfield in East Sussex as much as possible. It's the best kept secret, y'know."

For the first time, she felt a sense of belonging. She belonged to this conversation without the fear of saying or doing something inappropriate. In fact, Machiko couldn't remember the last time she had a real conversation with someone other than the Delacroix and their children.

Frankie possessed an endearing quirkiness with a maternal warmth that drew her in. A kind of comfort zone that she would have preferred from a parent, yet this woman was able to provide to her just by being in her company. The piercing ache shot through her and she choked back the yearning for those days when her own parents had loved her, had been proud of her.

Those days were dead and buried.

"Rotherfield sounds lovely. I'll have to visit for myself someday." She managed a cheerful smile.

"Tell me, have you met the neighbors yet?" Frankie asked nonchalantly while she picked up the teapot to refill the cups.

"Only one." The smoky voice answered from behind Machiko.

Her body tensed in awareness, all her senses screamed to attention. She had spent days trying to erase this man from her memory and it took seconds for all those images to come tumbling back. How could she possibly forget? Those brown eyes that could easily enchant her with their intensity.

Frankie's faces lit up in delight. "Caleb!" She scooted out of the chair and gave him a European-style greeting, kissing him affectionately on both cheeks. "So you've met our new visitor Mac, have you?"

Machiko rose slowly out of her chair, dreading to see *him* again. She wasn't prepared for the same electricity to surge through her body, the breathless need, the slow stirrings that spread to her sex.

"Fancy seeing you here," he teased.

"Yeah." She grunted.

Yeah? That one syllable word was the only thing she could respond!

How could she think straight when he looked so handsome in a fitted gray vintage *Sex Pistols* t-shirt and faded jeans? The sleeves hugged his biceps and she caught a hint of his tattoo peeking out from beneath the fabric of his left arm.

Men with tattoos had always been a lethal combination for her. A flash of memories re-surfaced from times past. She recalled that summer, almost a little over a decade ago, as clearly as it had just happened. She had barely turned eighteen, had left the wellness facility not more than a few months earlier when she decided to start her life again. The air had been hot and sticky when she headed for the train station with just the clothes on her back, a few personals in her backpack, and enough cash to get her on the bus headed to anywhere.

Machiko somehow wound up in Seattle and had taken a barista job at a cozy, underground café that hosted musical events. They were desperate for help and her appearance and demeanor had been exactly what they were looking for. Her three-month stint had led to her first lover.

His eyes were like polished jade. His dark hair and Scottish burr lured her in like the seductive songs he sang. There was nothing nice about him and his interest in her only heightened his sexiness. He was seven years older, ran with the wrong crowd, had a way with making her body feel things she wasn't certain about.

Green Eyes waited for her shift to end and followed her into the alley. He hadn't spoken a word to her except for the occasional small talk. She had been unprepared for his kiss and her body's reaction. They didn't need words for what he had in mind and their sexual heat spoke volumes that night. She had lost her virginity to him on the hand-me-down mattress in her cramped studio apartment.

She had woken up to an empty bed. His scent still lingered on her skin and she knew it would the last time she would ever see him again. He was the beginning of her metamorphosis, the paint trail that led her to the cravings. He propelled her need to grasp for the explosion of colors fighting for release from her soul. Green Eyes had showed her a world she had only imagined, been curious about, and the results had led her to a profound curiosity. Led her to a quest for understanding and conquering the powers of sensuality.

Caleb shifted from one foot to the other and the sound broke Machiko from her reverie.

His crooked smile sent a delicious shiver rippling through her. "Are you all settled in?"

She nodded, giving him a forced smile. "As settled as a housesitter can be."

"That's good. Very good…" his voice trailed off. Was the man at a loss for words? Somehow he didn't strike her as a person who would be in this predicament.

Frankie blurted cheerfully, "I'll go grab another cup for you. Have a seat, my dear boy, and keep Mac company." She patted his cheek and dashed off before Machiko could have a chance to protest.

They stood in silence.

Say something.

No words would come when he gazed at her with such unwavering focus. As if she were a complex canvas for which he studied, drawing details from his observations of her for insight into her mind. A Jackson Pollack with all the chaos intertwined within splatters. Splatters consisting of pain, sorrow, anger, fear. Yet the one missing element she craved most would not be present…*love*.

A shiver ran through her. Would she ever know this absent component in her lifetime?

Caleb cleared his throat and she snapped back to the present. "Have you had a chance to see the sites? Manhattan Beach has some spectacular views and a few interesting places to dine at."

Machiko couldn't stop staring at his lush lips. She wanted to run her fingers across them, wanted to feel the shape and lines. She wondered how they would taste, or feel pressed against hers. Her lips tingled at the notion. "I wouldn't know. I have been a bit…preoccupied."

Her eyes moved upwards with slow deliberation, locking with his, a spark of interest gleamed within the clear brown depths. His reaction slapped her back to attention. An overwhelming sense of embarrassment stained her cheeks and panic seized her.

"I...I've got to go. I've got to go." The words tumbled out and the horror she felt added to her need to leave. She ran past him without another glance, ran down the steps, never stopping until she reached her house.

She hadn't heard him calling her name, hadn't realized he was following closely behind her. Machiko could only think about getting away from these emotions that have been consuming her since those dreams. When the blurred face of her dream lover started to materialize and morphed into *his*.

The desire to smother the image had been so difficult that she tried to stay awake just to ensure she would be too tired to dream. His touch, his body, his face became all too real and when faced with him in the flesh, the reality was overwhelming to her senses.

Her heart raced, her chest grew heavy and all she wanted was to lock herself in the house, her secret place where she could hide away from these temptations that haunted her.

Were the temptations a need for something she denied herself for fear of letting others too close? She shoved the sliding glass doors apart, not quite making it past the threshold when strong fingers wrapped around her forearm. Stopping her from any chance of reaching her sanctuary.

"Whoa...why are you running, Mac? What are you running from?" His rich voice was filled with concern.

I'm running from you! Machiko's conscience screamed. She took in a deep breath to calm herself. The moments ticked away and she knew the best thing to do was to face him. His hold burned her flesh and launched a fiery path blazing down into her abdomen.

She took a deep breath and turned to face him. "What am I running from? I ran because...*I want you.*"

Chapter Three

Did he hear her correctly? This beautiful creature didn't hesitate to tell him what she wanted. Straightforward and to the point, except for her ability to maintain a conversation. Still, her odd behavior suggested something of a challenge to unearth. Something he would take pleasure in discovering.

Who was this woman? And why did he find her so fascinating?

I want you. The words echoed through him, teasing a soft spot in his soul. How could one respond to something so candid, yet so vulnerable? She was a pocketful of surprises that was both refreshing and admirable.

He watched her dark eyes, as beautiful as black satin, glittering with expectation as she waited for him to react. Her youthful face was filled with innocence, untouched by makeup. Mac was nothing like the type of women in this town, where image was everything and looks could be bought without regard for the consequences. Did they not care that they would lose themselves in the process? The thought always bothered him and he hoped to God she wouldn't turn out like any one of those women in a year's time.

He drew in a deep breath and tried to maintain control. If she kept staring at him with those hungry, black eyes, he was liable to comply with her request. Deep down he knew it wasn't the right thing to do no matter how damn tempting.

"You don't mean that." He let go of her forearm, afraid that he might bruise her with his strength.

A flash of sadness flitted across her face as she spoke. "I'm not very good at this sort of thing." She dropped her gaze and her long, thick lashes shielded those gorgeous, exotic eyes from his view.

She lowered her voice, "I don't have a lot of experience with...*people*." The lyrical sound was like a summer breeze whispering into his ear.

Whether it was the scent of her cherry blossom perfume or the subtle sensuality of her movements, he didn't think, just reacted. Caleb reached out and gently nudged her chin up with his knuckles until he could look into her eyes.

"You're doing fine. Don't be afraid. I just want to be your friend. That's all."

She twisted her head out of his grasp.

"Friend? I don't need friends." Her eyes flashed angrily as if he had insulted her with his rejection.

Even in anger, she captivated him. Those eyes burned into his memory, those arresting almond-shaped eyes were a stark contrast to her golden skin set against jet-black, silky hair. The darkness made her features more prominent and so fucking desirable.

Caleb couldn't help memorizing every gorgeous inch of her petite frame. Would she fit perfectly in his arms, snuggled up against him? Soft, comfortable, so feminine. He let out a quick breath. Their closeness allowed him to have a clear view of those high cheekbones and luscious pouty lips. Her overall appearance pointed to a product of a mixed union, perhaps Japanese and European. He wasn't quite sure, but the combination made for a striking package.

Mac was undeniably in a whole different league than what he was used to. She dripped exoticism like the hybrid tea roses he planted with great care in his rooftop garden. These single blossom roses possessed all the virtues he looked for in a flower: delicate beauty, an intoxicating fragrance. She embodied these elements with a naturalness he couldn't seem to resist. However, beyond the physical he was drawn to her by an inexplicable connection he couldn't quite put a finger on.

Her reaction tripped an imaginary alarm in his head. "Who could have done this to you? Who made you build a wall so impenetrable around yourself?"

Mac's eyes widened then narrowed with icy coldness. "Why don't you just leave? Forget I said anything to you."

Her sudden change and defensive reaction pissed him off. "So you can lock yourself up in this house to hide from the world? You're going to have to face reality someday. Do you really want to live like this? Not everyone is out to hurt you. I won't hurt you."

She withdrew into her shell again and a part of him yearned to pull her into his arms, tell her everything would be okay. He couldn't help wondering who could have caused her so much pain.

Mac winced at his comment. She made him feel like a complete and total asshole. She balled her hands into fists at her side and lashed out, "Who the hell do you think you are to psychoanalyze me?"

God, she was stunning with those smothering eyes that showed a hint of irritation. For that matter, how could he refuse her when those succulent lips called to him like an open invitation? Her unconscious action appeared more provocative than it should be. His chest squeezed so tight and he was left with a hunger so intense he wanted to push her back against the glass doors and fuck her brains out.

But he wasn't that kind of guy, not with someone like her.

Caleb had a gut instinct that she wasn't anything like the women in this town. The vicious plastics that wanted to dig their claws into any man willing and able to provide them with all the luxuries they felt entitled to.

No, not her.

Mac radiated hurt like an injured bird that needed to be comforted, needed to be taken care of. Images of her weeping on the floor whirled in his head. The dull ache surged through him and he was compelled to touch her. She gasped when Caleb cupped her cheek.

He loved the feel of her creamy skin, couldn't resist running his thumb along her plump, lower lip. "Everyone needs a friend. Even you," his voice came out huskier than he intended.

"Please...please, don't," she begged.

For fuck's sake. Don't look at me with those eyes.

His cock swelled to life, his jeans suddenly a little too constricting. A slight breeze pushed past and he caught the scent of cherry blossoms and his imagination soared to new heights. Just the thought of her sprawled naked on a bed of crushed velvet sheets, her nipples taut, her body worshipped by a scattered spread of rose petals was enough to drive him mad with need.

Christ, he hadn't been this turned on in a long while. Caleb wanted her so bad he could almost taste her, sweet like ripe cherries dipped in chocolate.

He hadn't been prepared. He hadn't seen it coming. Mac opened her mouth like a blooming flower, taking his thumb into her mouth. He groaned at the unexpected warmth, the lazy swirl of her tongue on his flesh, and the sensations brought on a whole string of wicked thoughts. Was this how it would feel like to have her take him into her mouth? Indeed, Mac was pure heaven and a pinch of hell for torturing him in this way.

Not like this. Caleb shook off the lust-filled haze and dropped his hand. He stepped back to allow distance between them.

"Get in the house," he growled.

Caleb noticed her trembling at his instructions, could feel the heat growing between them and it made the situation more unbearable. "If you don't get in the house now, I'm afraid I'm going to do something we'll both regret."

"Caleb..."

"Just go inside, Mac."

A strange look washed over that naive face. Understanding

registered and she nodded, quickly slipping in between the glass doors.

She turned the lock and stood back, watching him, a vision framed behind the door staring back at him. A priceless painting held behind security glass: untouchable, unobtainable.

As he stared back, Caleb swore to himself all of this was going to change. He would break her out of those glass walls she had built around herself if it was the last thing he'd do.

◈◈◈

Machiko clamped the paintbrush between her teeth as she tried to figure out her latest piece. The running color scheme was shades of grey, the woman's dress deep scarlet. When she looked at the eyes she could feel the same hollowness reflecting in them.

Her fingers cramped up from her strong grip on the palette. She grabbed the brush and threw it into the jar of water in irritation. Flexing her hand, she could feel the tension dissolve. Her whole body seemed to be one big knot. Machiko blamed it on the bloody man who drove her to work herself into oblivion.

The sting of rejection had struck a sour chord in her confidence but she wasn't going to let the likes of him interfere with what she needed to do. Machiko tried to blow off the incident but she knew a week had passed and still no sign of him.

Yesterday she stopped in to see Frankie but she couldn't relax, always on edge that Caleb would pop in unexpectedly. After a brief visit, she made an excuse to leave. Obsessed, that's what she was. The man had a way with making her feel inadequate and it was starting to affect her work.

Every time she closed her eyes he would materialize like an apparition. Her mind kept returning to that damn tattoo. She was dying for a peek and wondered if he had others. What were they? What did they symbolize?

"Damn, him." She desperately needed a swim to wash away the man from her thoughts.

She glanced up at the Mondrian clock secured on the wall above the work station. Where did the time go? Already it was three in the morning and she was still wired from the coffee Frankie had given her.

She could feel the strain of her eyes. Machiko liked to create her paintings in layers. She would start up at least two or three paintings simultaneously. While one dried, she would start the second layer, and so on. Machiko had perfected this technique when she was eight and as the years passed, she had acquired a few other tricks to save time.

Tension clung to her like an invisible skin and she clasped her hands together, reaching up high above her head for a deep stretch. Still, that didn't help to expel her active mind.

Some air might be good for clearing the head. She decided to watch the sunrise, if she didn't fall asleep on the porch swing first. That didn't sound half bad. She padded across the room and out onto the wooden deck. The cool salty air instantly revitalized her.

She sucked in her breath at the breathtaking view of the ocean, sloshing and spilling across the smooth sand. The waters beckoned her in and she was seized with the overwhelming desire to cleanse herself. Perhaps then she could rid the impurities that affected her during her dream state.

Desperate times called for serious actions. Machiko unlatched the wooden gate and exited onto the granules of sand. Was she really doing this? Exhilarated by the spontaneity, she broke into a run down to the very edge of the sand. She pulled off her *Godsmack* t-shirt then discarded her faded denim cutoffs and underwear.

Standing naked beneath the darkened skies she could feel the powers of the earth and water. The cold morning air sent goose pimples across her flesh and every particle of her being awoken to nature's sweet cry. Sensual awareness cupped her breasts, caressed her body, teased her spirit with its loving seduction.

Machiko laughed and charged straight for the ocean, diving in before she could change her mind. As soon as she hit the icy water, she was chilled to the bone. Her body soon adjusted after a few minutes of being submerged but the instant shocked killed any emotion weighing on her.

She splashed around, swirling with the waves, allowing herself to enjoy the moment. Salt water licked at her lips, her face and she wandered back in time to a place buried in the recessed of her memory. A childish giggle escaped at remembering her father's strength as he threw her in the air, holding on tight so she would feel the security of his love.

He was a good father to her. Why the hell didn't she see it? Machiko closed her eyes, fighting back tears. She let the weight of the ocean carry her, sinking down, downward until she could shut out all the sounds in her head. She focused hard on colors, the only thing that mattered to her these days. Colors comforted her and gave her an escape from reality.

Caleb's words had hit a nerve and he was right. She didn't want to live a life hiding away, running. *No more running*. She needed to stop running before she drove herself right back to the facility that had cheated her out of a life of normalcy. Who could she blame except herself?

A loud splash caused ripples around her and she blinked to adjust to the darkness. Her eyes stung from the saltwater and before she could resurface she felt a strong arm wrap around her waist. They shot up so quickly she choked on the salty liquid on their way up.

Her temper boiled over at the stupidity of whoever was manhandling her. She pounded her hands against a solid chest while she used every cuss word that came to mind. When she was able to make out the person, could see the outline of the familiar face beneath the faint morning light, her anger turned to a blazing, fiery star of lust.

Chapter Four

Machiko clasped his face in her hands, planting a hard, angry kiss on his lips. He gasped at the unexpectedness of her action and she slipped her tongue between his lips, channeling all the heat that raged within her. When she felt his resistance melting away, she nipped at his lower lip, sucking gently on his flesh and he let out a low groan.

She wrapped her legs around his waist as Caleb kept them afloat. She enjoyed the feel of his mouth, his probing tongue, the way he explored her with the same feverish response. She was deep into the kiss when he pulled away, just enough to speak.

"We need to get back on shore before we both drown," his voice sounded hoarse as if he was trying to regain his composure.

You're a wanton fool, Machiko's conscience reminded her of her impulsive action. Humiliated by her body's response to Caleb, she quickly untangled her legs from his body and pushed him away, swimming with all her energy back to shore. She had always been a strong swimmer and spent many summers learning how to hold her breath under water for long stretches. How often had she wished to be a mermaid? Free to go wherever the currents carried her, never worrying about a society that did not understand or accept her.

She ran across the hard, wet surface, could feel the water splashing at her feet. When she reached the dry powdery sand and the tiny specks clung to her feet like a second skin. All she wanted to do was concentrate on distancing herself from him.

Machiko bent down and collected her clothes, clutching the material close to her body. She hated her inability for restraint; even in the wellness facility she had a penchant for reacting first. Always speaking her mind without anyone ever pointing out the repercussions of her actions. Bad habits die hard.

She straightened up ready to go when Caleb grabbed her waist, whirling her around to face him.

"Don't run," his voice was thick with emotion. "I'm not here to hurt you." He pulled her into his wet body, into his warmth. "I won't let anybody hurt you."

Machiko's heart pumped hard and fast at their closeness. She wanted to say so much, wanted to tell him to stay away from her so she didn't have to want him so much. She opened her mouth to speak but Caleb didn't give her the opportunity. He scooped her up into his arms, as if she was weightless, and carried her up the steps into the house.

She was shaking uncontrollably, perhaps from the early morning chill against her wet skin, or the fact that he was holding her so intimately. Caleb carried her in the direction of her bedroom, without hesitation, as if he knew where she slept at night. Had he been here before?

The Chinese lantern on her nightstand bathed the room in dim light, enough for her to see a profile of his handsome face. Machiko knew nothing about this man except that he had a knack for showing up whenever she didn't want him to.

She shifted her body, trying to capture his warmth, but the act made her more conscious of his muscles flexing as he walked. Awareness seeped in and every nerve ending lit up like rows of Christmas lights. She wrapped her arms tighter around herself and was swiftly reminded of her own nudity. A wave of embarrassment swept through her and she tried to struggle out of his hold.

"Don't fight me." He gripped her closer, almost as if he knew what she was thinking.

In her weary state she stopped fighting with Caleb. She settled back against him but warmth could not be found. Even when he placed her down at the edge of the bed she couldn't stop shivering. She was so cold, so numb from the icy emotions swirling inside and the loneliness of these past years. Machiko was torn between tears and laughter. She had never permitted herself to settle for weakness and in Caleb's arms she was compelled to unravel.

Caleb grabbed the comforter and placed it gently over her shoulders, pulling it tight around her to keep her warm. She continued to shake, unable to retain the heat. Her lips quivered and she couldn't control the chattering of her teeth.

"I'm going to find something to dry you off and then get you into something warm," he mumbled more for his benefit.

She didn't realize he had left the room until he returned with several large towels. With a skill and gentleness she didn't expect, he began the slow ministrations of drying her hair. His technique became a drug that lulled Machiko into giving into the sensations. She closed her eyes, reveling in the sensual, yet intimate act.

His touch was gentle as he rubbed her hair, massaging the scalp enough for it to feel arousing and soothing all at once. No one had ever been allowed this close to her before. Why Caleb? Her heart skipped and she knew the reasons even before her conscience responded. *Because he makes me feel safe*.

She opened her eyes, adjusting to the darkened room. She sucked in her breath at the sight of him, stripped of his own clothes, a towel hung snug around his waist. He stood so close to her, which gave her a clear view of his magnificent body.

He shifted his weight and the stream of light that had been blocked by his massive frame spilled through to reveal a gorgeous tattoo. She drank in the full details of the dragon's image, symbolizing grace and strength. The creature reminded her of the man standing before her. Its head rested on his upper pectoral muscle, the body spreading down his side and over his ribcage like a fluid ribbon. The dragon's tail curved around, ending just at the edge of his waist, yet the full display showcased the masterful brilliance of the artist.

The richness of the crimson, gold, and emerald colors against the intensity of the shading blended beautifully beneath the black ink. God, he turned her on. She wanted to run her tongue across his flesh and taste the explosion of colors in her mouth. The thought sent liquid lust coursing through her, down to the vee between her thighs.

She unconsciously reached out to trace the pattern with her fingers. Her forwardness made him tense up. He placed a hand over hers to stop the exploration. Caleb threw the towel he had used on her aside and cupped her cheek, gently nudging her head back so she could look up at him.

"I can't be a gentleman if you touch me. I'm only a man."

He studied her face and she saw desire shimmering in his eyes, could see his inner struggle.

Stay with me.

She didn't know if she could restrain herself from begging him to make love to her. She was desperate to feel again, to be wanted. Machiko needed a way to fill this void even for a night.

Caleb's voice came out rough, strained when he finally spoke. "Mac, this isn't what you want."

Silence.

She didn't want to break the spell. He made her feel like a woman tonight. Wanted. Beautiful. Sexy. Something she had never known before but now craved more.

"I'm going to help you into dry clothes and then I'm going to tuck you in." This time he sounded more controlled. Firm.

He dropped his hand and quickly turned away to rummage through her open closet. She didn't know what came over her but she wasn't going to back down now. *What do I have to lose?* He had already seen her naked and vulnerable.

She pushed the comforter off her shoulders to stand up, mentally preparing herself to face him. Would he reject her or fulfill her needs? Caleb turned, ready to speak but stopped dead in his tracks. He let out a deep sigh, fire blazing in his eyes.

He walked up to her, a cotton nightdress fisted tightly in his hand. Without saying a word he slipped the material over her head and helped her dress as if she were but a girl and not a woman. The dress barely covered her thighs but she was thankful it concealed her body from his view.

Humiliation stained her cheeks for a second time that night. Machiko was confused by his treatment of her. "Am I so undesirable you can't find yourself willing to make love to me?" The hurt was raw, excruciating as she waited for him to answer.

His eyes were impassive as he commanded, "Get under the covers."

"Caleb…"

"Shhh. Just do as I say."

When would she get it through her thick skull that he didn't want her? He had rejected her again. Shame washed through her body and she dropped her eyes, not ready to meet his gaze. They didn't speak as he helped her into the bed. When she was lying comfortably on the mattress, he pulled the comforter over her.

"I'll get my clothes from your dryer and will lock the door after." He said softly before turning to leave.

"Stay with me." She hadn't meant to say it out loud, couldn't take back the words now.

He stiffened at her request and she prayed the floor would open up and suck her down a black hole. Seconds ticked on as she waited for him to speak. *Say anything, dammit!*

The silence stretched on and all she could do was stare at the curve of his back, the cords of his muscles taut across his shoulders. He would be the perfect subject to paint. Would that be enough for her?

She could study him freely now that his backside was to her. His body was well-defined by the dim glow from the early morning sun pushing its way through. Her nipples hardened at the sight of another tattoo adorning his body. This time it was an exquisite image of a Phoenix in mid-flight. The tattoo matched the width and height of the dragon that resided on the front of his body. The bird's feather touched the tail of the dragon in an almost sensual way.

Strength and rebirth. The union of opposites.

Her eyes drifted away from the Phoenix to his left bicep. Just as she imagined for days now, he had a sorcerer's band. This Celtic interlaced armband was like the mesmerizing words of a powerful spell, an intricate braidwork of knots and tangles that connected to the beginning, symbolizing infinity of power.

He definitely had powers over her.

She waited for a response that she believed would never come.

Please stay with me.

Caleb swore under his breath and turned back around, sliding under the covers beside her. He reached for her and pulled her body to him, his strong arms secure around her waist.

"Now, go to sleep," his command gruff, yet gentle at the same time.

A smile formed on her lips. She thought back to the ocean and his earlier reaction. She wondered if he had assumed she was drowning out there. Perhaps that was the reason he jumped in to try and rescue her. Would anyone else have done so?

Machiko snuggled back against him, her head cradled by the curve of his neck. She needed this. She would take what she could, if he was willing to give it. This would have to be enough for her and would fill those lonely days ahead.

When she inhaled, his scent filled her head, a natural musk mixed with saltwater. She wanted to lock away the memory of this moment. His touch made her think of being a butterfly wrapped in a tight cocoon. Warm, secure, safe.

There had only been a handful of men in her life and none made her feel this way, except for Caleb. Right here, right now she had been more comfortable than she had ever experienced. He was hardly more than a stranger, yet she couldn't deny the attraction, the invisible force throwing them together, the instant connection. In all her years she could not remember a instant like this or with a man quite like him.

Yes, she was safe. His arms were her haven and his touch her kryptonite. He had told her he didn't want to hurt her and she believed him. Machiko had never trusted anyone before and this man was slowly inching through her barrier.

She didn't want to think anymore. Her lids grew heavy, tired from the events of the morning. His soft breathing was like a lullaby luring her to sleep and soon the questions swimming in her head quickly dissolved, drifting into the darkness.

She smelled so damn good. Caleb inhaled the cherry blossom scent mixed with salt and sea. She fit perfectly, her petite frame molded so well against his body. This was the first time he had slept with a woman without trying to seduce her. There was something about Mac that made things seem surreal, magical almost.

The past week had been excruciating knowing she was so close yet off limits. He couldn't go five minutes without thinking about her and now he had her in his arms. Jesus, the way her ass wiggled up against his dick was wreaking havoc on his libido. If she didn't stop he was going to throw proper etiquette out the window and be the heathen he really was.

Concentrate, man!

Caleb leaned into her hair, still moist even after he had tried toweling it dry. She was finally asleep. Her soft breathing sounded like a sweet caress and he closed his eyes to focus in on the sound. He had stayed permanently hard since the first day he laid eyes on her, and even as he held her now, he wanted her so bad he thought he'd snap from the pain.

There had been plenty of opportunities in the past when he held a beautiful woman in his arms, and frankly, sleeping wasn't on his mind. Holding Mac now, he found her so comfortable, couldn't bring himself to disrupt this moment. The thought scared him shitless, more from the fact that he was already half crazy wanting her and trying his best not to want her.

Shit, he wasn't making any sense right now.

With Mac, there was something so alluring, so frustrating and unpredictable about her that kept him desperate to figure her out. He was afraid if he gave in and slept with her there would be awkward tension between them. How could he face Luc if he had casual sex with her and broke her heart? That could pose a problem for everyone.

She stirred, moaning in her sleep, rubbing back against him and he gnashed his teeth together. Jesus, he needed to focus on something other than running his hands over her tight little body. Her hand reached for his, and in her sleep induced state, she pushed his hand down between her thighs to cover her mound. He had forgotten she wasn't wearing underwear beneath her gown and he could feel the heat radiating off of her. His fingers tangled in her curls and his self-control came crashing down around him.

Even in sleep she still wanted him. This knowledge pleased him in a strange sadistic way. He swallowed hard and made a quick decision. Hell, one of them should get some satisfaction. Why not her? He parted her delicate flesh with his fingers. Imagining how sweet she would taste on his lips. She was already wet and ready for him, and so fucking hot.

He rubbed his thumb across her hardened clit and she let out a soft moan. His shaft grew rigid against the towel, the barrier between his body and hers. Christ, he wanted inside. He slipped a finger into her slick heat and bit back his own urge to lick the honeyed sweetness. He slid in another finger and her moan escalated.

He was determined to make her come. He started to pump into her with slow ease. He slid his fingers out, pumping back in with a rhythm that she seemed to enjoy. She squirmed, her excitement building, her breathing faster. Her breasts grazing his arm, her nipples hard and asking to be sucked.

He kept the momentum by increasing the tension. She was uninhibited, grinding against his hand. Her response was so fucking hot he probably didn't need to fuck her to come. He continued pumping into her, applying pressure on her clit and her moans became almost unbearable for him. When he felt she was ready to be taken over the edge, he flicked his thumb across her tiny pearl and she let out a loud cry as she climaxed. He could feel her body tremble, shaking from the aftershock, growing limp from the aftermath.

Only then did he realize her nails had dug into his thigh, almost deep enough to draw blood. He didn't give a damn as long as he was the drug that would keep her sedated. He may not have made love to her but the pleasure he had just given her was well worth the frustrated days that loomed ahead for him. When he was certain she had fallen back into a deep sleep, he allowed himself to finally relax.

Yet sleep never came to him.

⊗✻◈

Caleb watched his younger sister Gemma's animated expression as she gave him a recap of her work week over lunch. They sat outside on the patio at Poseidon's Net, an Oceanside café, their usual hangout to catch up on the events in their lives.

While he listened, he couldn't shake the images of Mac from his head, especially what he had done to her, or what he had wanted to do to that luscious body. When he left her house this morning he felt a tinge of guilt nipping at his insides.

Would it be awkward for her to face him? He hoped not. She was like an addiction and he planned on seeing her as often as possible. He needed to.

"Well, are you coming?" Gemma's irritated tone intruded his thoughts.

"About what?"

"C'mon. I can't believe you didn't hear me." Her face beamed with excitement. "I was asking about you attending my great shoe line unveil. Are you able to attend this Saturday to support me?"

His eyebrows shot up in surprise. "Serious? That's fantastic, sis!"

Gemma gave him a wide grin. "You aren't such a dumb oaf after all."

"Do you think I can get a preview of the catering menu? I'm

only there for the food."

She punched him in the arm. "That's all?"

"Oh. For you, too," he teased.

Her cell rang and she gave him a dirty look before picking up.

He watched her, a sense of pride welled up inside. She was growing into a beautiful young woman with a solid career path. He couldn't believe, not long ago, she wore pigtails and clung to Barbie dolls. Being ten years older than her, there had always been a wide gap that separated them.

Caleb and Gemma were definitely night and day. From the outside world she looked nothing like him, yet their sibling bond was unbreakable. The drastic differences didn't stop at their looks. Where he had dark hair and eyes, she was blonde with blue eyes. Where he was laid back and easy going, she was a control freak with a meticulous attitude toward everything she did.

He lived for these lunch dates with his sister. This had become a weekly ritual when he had purchased his house five years ago. Gemma was newly graduated, a shoe designer with dreams of becoming a household name like Manolo Blahnik or Jimmy Choo. She would crash at his house on the weekends to get away from her roommates in order to complete projects required for her internship.

At twenty, she was overly ambitious, too mature for her own good. Her future was bright, secure. That's when everything went to hell in a hand basket. She was offered a job at Courtney Morgan, a rising shoe company where she had a brief and scandalous affair with Morgan. Even now, the thought of that asshole made him cringe, ready to beat the living shit out of the guy.

The end result? Gemma became pregnant at twenty-two, her career in limbo, her heart in pieces. Caleb couldn't watch as his sister fell apart and had stepped in. He became the big brother she deserved. He picked her back up, annoyed the hell out of her, and got her back on track.

Now four years later she had worked her way back up from

anonymity into becoming one of the most sought after young designers in California.

Gemma used her calming mommy voice, "That's right Jonah, mommy will be home soon. I love you, too." She completed the call, snapped the phone shut, and placed the phone on the table.

"Sorry about that."

"No worries. How's the little guy, anyway? I thought I'd take him off your hands sometime next week if it's okay." He tried to be a good uncle and spent as much time with his nephew as possible.

"You kidding? That'll be great. Four-year-olds are more than a handful and I've got some client meetings on Thursday. How about then?" She leaned in, a devilish twinkle in her eyes. "Now, about Saturday. Who are you taking?"

He knew that look. She was up to no good.

"You'll just have to find out."

She pouted. "What? Aren't you taking Jordan?"

"Gems, we've split up two years ago or haven't you noticed."

"She's always gone to functions with you." She wrinkled her nose at him. "You don't have to get all touchy about it."

Caleb picked up his iced tea and took a healthy swallow. "Just be glad I'm coming. You can invite her separately if you really want her to show."

The server dropped off their lunches and Gemma grabbed her fork, digging into her cobb salad. "Fine. You know how long it took for me to like someone you're dating? Now I'm going to have to go through this all over again."

He smiled as he speared a green bean from his nicoise salad. "She's new in town and a friend of Luc's."

"A sympathy date?" She raised a brow at him.

"No! I thought it would be nice because she's a little shy. Probably doesn't get out much." He shuffled his food around before spearing a big bite of the salad.

Maybe shy was an understatement, but he thought Mac needed to leave the house. He wanted her to experience the Los Angeles fashion scene. These parties were organized much like a gallery showing and he figured she would be more in her element.

"I swear if I'm stuck in the bathroom all night trying to console her after you've broken her heart, I will hunt you down like a dog..." she muttered the rest incoherently.

He rolled his eyes. "I got the point. Send the damn invitation and I'll be there. Is this black tie or can I roll in with jeans and flip-flops?"

"So help me! Why did I have to have you as a brother?"

Caleb enjoyed egging her on and today was no exception. In the back of his mind he was counting down the minutes before he showed up at her door. What woman wouldn't want to be asked to attend one of the most exclusive events of the season?

Chapter Five

Caleb felt like an idiot as he stood outside Machiko's front door. Her irritated expression made him wish he had waited to spring it on her.

"You're taking me where?" Mac pursed her lips.

He wanted to wrap his hand around that tiny neck of hers for giving him the third degree. He ran his hand through his hair, already annoyed by her abrupt change in attitude. "At least let me in so we can discuss this."

She folded her arms, speaking in the same controlled manner, "From what I'm hearing, you've already committed me."

"I thought it'd be…"

She turned on her heel and walked away. *Just like that.*

He clenched his jaw so tight he thought he would get a headache from it. "Where are you going?"

Caleb entered the house and shut the door behind him. He followed her to the kitchen, watching her pull out a large bottle of Perrier from the fridge before slamming it shut with her hip.

He couldn't deny she made a pretty picture in a ginger-colored, backless summer dress that tied around her neck. His groin jerked when he got a good eyeful of her toned legs and calves. She stretched, standing on tiptoes as she pulled two glasses off the shelf. His eyes slid down to her ankles. He sucked in his breath at seeing the tiny lotus blossom tattoo displayed on her left ankle.

His heart did a quick drop when she whirled around and placed the glasses on the island counter. She twisted off the Perrier cap and he watched with fascination as she poured the fizzy liquid into one glass, then the other. Mac set the bottle back down, grabbed a glass and handed it to him.

She spoke in an unemotional tone, "Look, this might be a bit awkward for you but I'm not interested in you in *that* way."

He shot her an incredulous look. "Are you kidding me? You've practically been throwing yourself at me since we first met."

"Exactly. I just want sex. I don't want the complication that goes with dating or a relationship."

He grabbed the glass and downed the drink, all while eyeing her with contempt. "I'm trying to be nice to you and you think I want to date you? C'mon, I'm not that desperate." Caleb scoffed and she poured another hefty portion into his glass.

"I'm assuming what you did to me the other day might have given you the ammo to want something more—er, permanent." She sipped her drink, her gaze unwavering.

She had balls, he'd give her that. She had spoken her mind without appearing unruffled or embarrassed. Still, her reaction didn't sit well with him. Did he mean *nothing* to her?

"We're not in high school here. You asked for some release and I gave it to you. Period. End of story."

Mac grabbed his unfinished drink from him.

"Hey, I wasn't done with that."

She carried the glasses to the sink, poured out the contents and placed the empty glasses inside.

"Well, I'm done with you." There was a cool edge to her voice.

Again, she didn't give him a chance to continue the conversation before heading out of the kitchen to the front of the house. She yanked the door open and waited for him to leave, her hand tightly gripping the doorknob.

He shook his head. She was a strange mix of odd and insufferable. He didn't know when he had ever been so charged up in a conversation. Caleb was normally even-tempered and laid back yet Mac kicked the Zen out of him since their first encounter.

What was her problem? She acted as if she had never had a friend before; and who would want to be friends with a moody, pain in the ass girl-woman?

He stood beneath the threshold, turning to face her, needing to get the last word in. "Is this a trust issue? I told you not everyone is out to get you and if you would give me a chance you'd see that I'm a nice guy."

She spat, "Trust? You don't even know my last name and you're asking me to trust you." She pushed at his chest and he stepped back, teetering out the door. "I'm not sure I even like you." She pushed him again and when he stumbled out the door she tried shutting it on him.

Caleb wasn't giving up without at fight. He stuck his foot out and the door bounced open. He asked in a clipped tone, "So, are you gonna go with me or not?"

◌

Machiko pounded on the door. She couldn't believe she was standing in front of Caleb's house and she couldn't believe she was about to tell him she had decided to go with him to the lousy shoe party.

She waited impatiently. Frustrated, she pounded on the door again and pressed the doorbell a few times for good measure.

The door swung open.

"What the fu—," Caleb frowned upon seeing her. She gave him her most pleasant smile, one she had practiced in front of the mirror a dozen times before heading over.

"Aren't you going to invite me in?" She didn't wait to hear his answer and ducked under his arm, walking past him into the living room.

She hadn't expected his house would be very minimalistic, elegantly decorated in warm browns, reds, and beiges. Several surfboards were propped against a wall near the patio. She hadn't expected anything less. Machiko scanned the room to check out the rest of his environment.

Simple, organized, uncomplicated. Unfortunately, nothing like the man. She bit her lower lip to hide a smile that threatened to surface.

"To what do I owe the pleasure?" He walked over to stand beside her.

She twisted around, unprepared to find him shirtless. Her mouth suddenly dry. She couldn't help assessing his body, her eyes roaming over his figure. Tough, lean, well-developed. His physique was an artist's dream and she craved to paint him as much as she craved to lure him into her bed.

Her sex swelled at the image of them rolling around in the paints. She became moist with excitement.

Caleb placed his hands on his hips. "I know it must have been difficult for a hermit like you to leave the cave. So, why are you here?"

Her attention was soon drawn to the dragon tattoo that moved with him. In the light, the details popped out, appearing even more incredible than when she had first seen it. The Japanese style design was so pure and exotic, reminding her of a long forgotten traditional artistry. A chill coursed through her and she dragged her eyes away and tried to feign interest in his house, his collection of artwork.

She had to admit the man had good taste in art. Beautifully framed life-sized paintings decorated his walls and she even recognized a few notable artists. Machiko glanced around the expanse of the room, her eyes immediately lured to a place above the fireplace. One particular painting leapt out at her and she stepped in for a closer look. This painting was Chagall's *Three Candles!*

Soft light poured across the painting from a sturdy track light. A slick conical design. The way the painting was displayed, as well as the rest of the art pieces, made her realize

Caleb wasn't any normal collector. He was an art lover. Her stomach fluttered and she had a newfound respect for the man.

"You're familiar with Marc Chagall?"

She was speechless, could only nod. She tilted her neck back for a better observation. Mac knew that these paintings were rare, almost impossible to possess, and it occurred to her she really knew nothing about Caleb's background. Perhaps it wasn't a bad thing to learn more about him.

She squinted, focusing fully on the painting. From her experience, she could spot a print from the real deal and *this* was no replica. But how could someone like him own such a prize?

She swung around, her gaze resting on his. "Three Candles?" She wrinkled her nose at him. "It's one of my favorite pieces. Chagall's trademark themes run through it. Young love, religious icons, with a mix of his abstract style."

He rubbed his jaw and a half smile crossed his face. "Tell me, what do you like most about his work?"

"I am inspired by a man who has a true appreciation of love. You can tell that he has respect and dignity for this emotion just by looking at it." She pointed at the painting, elation filled her heart. Art was a language she could relate to, could speak without fear or reservations.

"You see the clarity of the candles as well as the couple? See how they seem to be rising with the angels? Notice the elements around them appear to be in a dreamlike state."

"Yes, I see that." He stepped in closer and kept his gaze on her.

She cocked her head back and looked up at the painting, still in awe as she spoke, "The colors are so vivid, so personal as if he's here telling me the story. Not many people will ever get the same message but it doesn't matter. It only matters that I understand."

He placed a hand on her shoulder. "Tell me, why are you here?"

Machiko took a deep breath, looking at him through her lashes. "I've decided to go with you."

"And what if I've changed my mind?" His voice a caress as his hand slid down her arm, sending a wave of pleasure through her.

"You can't change your mind."

His fingers stopped at the tender flesh at her wrist, right below her palm. "I can't go with someone who doesn't trust me."

She withdrew, moving away from him, from his touch. "Give me a reason to trust you."

He threw up his hands in the air. "Name it. Anything and I'll do it because I want you to know I'm putting my trust in you. Is that good enough?"

A few loose tendrils fell across her eye and Machiko tucked them behind her ear. *Think, think.* She smoothed her hair, reaching into the recesses of her mind for something, anything that would jump out at her. Nothing would come. She blew out an exasperated breath, fixing her eyes on him. There was an inherent strength in his face that was growing on her.

He gave her a smile that reached his eyes, sending her pulse racing. Damn him and those compelling toffee eyes! Damn his firm, sensual lips she couldn't wait to kiss again!

Nervously she moistened her dry lips.

"What do I need to do?" His tone was huskier than she remembered. The smile in his eyes contained a sensuous flame and heat rose to her cheeks.

Her eyes moved to a spot above his head and something clicked. She zeroed in on his thick mass of dark hair and an idea sprang to life.

Somehow he understood her expression. He shook his head, his eyes widened in alarm. "Oh, no. You're fucking kidding me?" He thrust his fingers through his hair, massaging his scalp as if it was already as good as gone.

Machiko gave him a lazy smile, nodding slowly and with emphasis. If he allowed her to do as she wished, she would be convinced he was serious about trusting her. This was the only way. She wanted to trust him.

Barging past him, she went in search of the bathroom and

after several wrong tries she managed to find one.

"How many bathrooms does a guy really need?" she muttered under her breath as she pulled the cabinets open, one by one. She rummaged through the drawers until she found what she was looking for. *Aha!*

Her heart hammered against her chest, her hand shaking as she unzipped the black leather case. She should feel some sort of guilt but she didn't. Machiko pulled out the heavy electric razor with a built-in trimmer and powered it up. She swallowed the lump in her throat.

His hair would grow back in no time at all.

Caleb stepped inside the bathroom and the soft hum made him pause at the door. She gave him a wicked grin as she held up the buzzing razor. "Do you trust me?"

He couldn't fucking believe what she was about to do, or the fact that he had instigated this. Of course he should be freaking out but a sick part of him found the idea thrilling. Not because his hair was coming off, more in knowing that Mac was the one doing the honors.

Caleb had never cut his hair shorter than business appropriate. He often grew his hair out during the summer months when he surfed and didn't give two licks what people thought of him. Never had it crossed his mind to shave his head.

Fuck it! If this was what he needed to do to gain Mac's trust, he was going to bite the bullet and do it.

He inhaled a lungful of air and walked over to her.

Do or die.

She let out a shriek when he grabbed her waist with both hands and plopped her down on the counter. Reaching for the razor, he flipped the metal object over to the trimmer side before placing it back in her palm. She trembled and he wondered if she had a change of heart.

"First things first. You want trust, let's get the formalities out of the way. Caleb Holden," he gave her a devilish grin.

She rolled her eyes but went with it. "Machiko Barrett."

"Right." Caleb sucked in his breath. He closed his hand over hers and without blinking he guided the trimmer to his hairline.

His eyes clung to hers in silent communication. He felt the blood coursing through his veins like an awakened river. This was the most intimate moment in his life and he was sharing it with Machiko. A woman he could barely tolerate but also unable to stay away from. She was real good. She managed to invade his private domain based on one weak moment.

If he hadn't seen her that morning a few weeks ago they wouldn't be in this surreal predicament. When was the last time he let anyone this close to him? Not since his father died, not since he had to become a man before he was ready to. His stomach squeezed at the painful reminder.

The razor hummed steadily as it skimmed across his scalp in one straight line. His dark locks fell noiselessly to the floor around him. Mac gasped in initial shock, shutting off the razor. They were wrapped in complete silence, their gazes locked for what seemed like an eternity, and he thought he could heard the faint beating of her heart. Or was that his own heartbeat?

Her expression was a total turnabout. A sensual smile curved her lips and she looked as if she was basking in the knowledge of her power. God, she was stunning. His eyes slid down her face, to the creamy expanse of her neck, lower to her perky breasts that were barely covered by the thin dress.

He was rock hard again. His imagination spurred on by weeks of unfulfilled need. What he would give to bend her back against the mirror, lift up her dress and taste her honeyed sweetness. Part of him wanted to put them both out of their misery once and for all.

Didn't she tell him she only wanted sex? What was the harm in that? Every muscle in his body tightened in defiance. His conscience stopped him from letting his dick take the lead on this one. If he gave in it would only compromise his intentions. Fine damn time for him to have a conscience!

His eyes traveled back up to her face and he discovered a hint of sadness lingering in her onyx depths. Had it always been there before? Those sad eyes cloaked beneath long, thick lashes. He had a gut feeling he was over his head but there was something alluring and mysterious about her that made things interesting.

Why her? What made her so different from the other women he had pursued in the past?

She's like the lotus blossom tattooed on her ankle. So delicate beneath the hardened coat of paint that shields her from the world yet she possesses a strength you haven't found in others, that's what. His inner voice pointed out.

Did his brain cells go with his hair? Hell, they had known each other a handful of weeks now and he was still trying to dissect everything. This head-shaving stunt was probably a game to her but he honestly believed she wanted his friendship. He'd never seen a person in need of a friend more than Mac. Her eyes, her expression, her tone screamed for someone to protect her. Befriend her.

Yes, that was the reason he was letting her shave his head. He wanted to gain her trust. The only reason he would go through such pains.

Caleb caught his reflection in the antique mirror behind her. Not a pretty sight but he'd have to get used to it for a few weeks until it grew out. There was no turning back now.

In all honesty, when he had watched his hair come off it was almost a freeing act, a spiritual awakening. He felt it. Felt the deep connection that surged between them and he wondered if it was all conjured up in his head from the exhilarated state. Did she feel it too?

Even if she didn't feel a thing, he had just helped her make the first indentation and possibly a lasting impression in her stubborn little head.

"Trust me now?"

She didn't speak; the smile she gave him was as intimate as a kiss.

Time to get the rest over with and have her finish the job. He got up off the floor and she placed a hand on his forearm. She eased him around to face in the direction of the door. Caleb understood what she wanted and returned to the kneeling position. His knees were pressed against the cold ceramic floor and reminded him of penance. He wanted to laugh. Was this payback for all the hearts he had broken along the way?

Mac scooted forward, her thighs closing around his ribcage, her legs dangling on each side of him. Her tiny hand shot around him and he hadn't expected the firm grip on his chin as she gently tilted his head back against her breast. He heard her flip on the switch and the buzzing resumed.

Her actions were gutsy, powerful, erotic.

She had a steady grip and her movements were precise as she clipped the rest of his hair off with the trimmer. Mac turned off the razor and placed it on the counter.

She ran her hand across his head, massaging lightly before she let go of his chin. "I think I'm not completely satisfied."

Caleb twisted his head to see her. "What?"

"You heard me. I want it all off." Her dark eyes gleamed with a sensual cruelness.

"Completely?"

She gave him a seductive smile. "Every bit of it."

"You're sadistic, Mac. You know that?" He stood up and his knees throbbed from kneeling on the hard floor. He quickly retrieved the shaving cream and disposable razor from the medicine cabinet and handed it to her. He had never see such pure happiness shine on someone's face as he did hers.

"I'll need a towel," she added.

He grabbed the hand towels from a metal towel rack and dropped it next to her.

"Resume position please." She batted her lashes and he didn't know whether he wanted to kiss her or strangle her.

No, he did not like the enjoyment she was receiving at his expense. Once again he found himself facing the door and his first inclination was to run before it was too late. He had to smile at the absurdity of the events leading up to this point.

All thoughts flew out the window when Mac brushed her fingers across his neck, caressing his skin. She parted her thighs and he leaned back into her. The dress had crept up and he could feel the warmth of her skin as she wrapped her legs around his chest. Flesh on flesh.

He could feel her feminine heat against his back and he clenched his jaw to suppress the urges threatening to resurface.

"Make it quick," he ground out.

Her charming laughter helped him relax. Being with her right now filled him with contentment and he wrapped his arms around her legs, as if they had been this intimate a hundred times before. He stroked the smooth flesh, enjoying the feel of her toned legs as he waited.

He could feel her reaching back, heard the turn of the faucet, then the gush of running water. Wet hands touched his head and he melted beneath her fingers. Another second later she had popped the top off the shaving cream and he listened to the soft swoosh of the foam. She lathered his head with slow, sensual strokes as she quickly finished her chore.

She pressed the razor against his skin and he felt the sharp instrument glide easily across his scalp. With every stroke, energy flowed through him, pushing him closer to Machiko.

Chapter Six

Machiko leaned against the patio door watching Frankie dancing and singing along to Stevie Nick's *Landslide*. Her soothing tone and the clarity and strength of her vocals hinted to a professional singing background, or many years of training.

She loved the older woman's vivacious spirit and was glad she made the decision to drop by unannounced. During the past few weeks she had the opportunity to get to know her neighbor better and their relationship somehow morphed into an extended family situation.

Machiko didn't know much about fashion and as Saturday approached she hoped Frankie would be able to help her in this department. The woman obviously had distinct taste in clothes based on her current attire. She grinned at the picture-perfect display. Frankie's bright tunic dress flowed with her as she used the feather duster on the rust-colored antique shelf, navigating around picture frames and miniature glass figurines.

Mac tapped on the side of the door and Frankie straightened up, giving her a bright smile.

"Hello, darling! What a pleasant surprise to see you. Come on in." She tucked the feather duster on the shelf and walked over to greet Mac with a hug and kiss on the cheek.

"Spring cleaning or simply bored?"

Frankie laughed. "I thought I'd do it myself. Usually Adia comes by three times a week to help me straighten up a bit but I gave her the day off. Say, how about some nicely chilled raspberry iced tea? I was just going to get myself a glass."

"Sounds refreshing." Mac followed her into the Spanish-style kitchen.

She had been in this room a handful of times but she always loved the coziness of the kitchen. What a vast difference from the Delacroix contemporary, sleek and clean design. This kitchen possessed a dramatic space that combined classic arts-and-crafts style with modern functionality and natural light.

The floor was made of grainy tiles and provided a rustic feel reminiscent of the Old World. Floral designs were hand-painted on tiles that made a striking pattern on the breakfast counters and over the sinks. The glassware was placed in cabinets with French doors while hanging pots and pans were hooked on metal racks affixed on the wall.

Frankie went about gathering the iced tea and glasses and Mac settled down at the dinette table.

"You finished painting already? Or just taking a break?" Frankie handed her the drink.

"Actually, I was hoping to get some advice. Maybe some help." The older woman slid in the chair across from her.

"Anything for you. What is the 4-1-1?"

The early morning breeze blew through the open windows and temporarily tamed the rising temperature in the kitchen but not enough to quench the awkward request she was about to make.

Mac sipped her iced tea and a refreshing cold rush streamed through her system, taking the edge off of the hot summer day. She couldn't look Frankie in the eyes, a little embarrassed about having to ask someone for help on short notice. Why did she wait so long? She focused on the droplets of perspiration on the glass.

"Caleb asked me to some shoe event and I don't really know

what one wears to these functions."

Frankie let out an excited squeal, "That's fantastic! I would love to help you choose a dress. When is the event?"

She gave her a smirk. "Tonight."

"Heavens! We best get moving. Drink up, dear."

◦✣◦

Blinking once, then twice, Machiko didn't recognize the person staring back at her. She stood on a platform in front of an oversized folding mirror, studying herself from three different angles. No matter which way she looked at it she still couldn't believe the woman in the mirror was she.

The marathon had begun as soon as she said the word "tonight". Frankie had literally dragged her out the door and taken her to an exclusive boutique on Rodeo Drive. The older woman had dialed several places and begged for favors while she maneuvered through the chaotic morning traffic. They had made it to the shop in one piece and Machiko had wanted to drop to the ground and kiss the asphalt parking lot.

The day had zipped by and she had endured the makeover mayhem. Exhausted, numb and overloaded by the blurs of faces and names Machiko didn't think she would make it through the day. She had met more people in one morning than she had in the nine years as an au pair. Her anxiety had reached a new level, but Frankie had been there every step of the way to ease her tensions.

"You're absolutely stunning." Frankie beamed like a proud pageant mom.

"She's gorgeous. This dress was made for her." Donovan Blake, an elegant brunette with classic features and a supermodel's body, stepped closer to the platform and adjusted the draping on the gown. "I knew this dress would be perfect for someone someday. I'm so glad I didn't try to re-design it. I didn't have the heart to." Donovan straightened up to admire the creation.

The gown was a custom designed piece from a private

collection for a celebrity client. At the last minute the woman had changed her mind and the dress had remained forgotten in the back room for a few weeks. She was grateful Donovan had offered the evening gown to her.

Machiko's eyes never left the view of her reflection. Rapture and nervousness swirled in her stomach and she imagined this was how Cinderella felt before attending the ball. She was astonished that a professional grooming session could turn someone as plain as herself into a beauty.

Smoke and mirrors.

She couldn't stop smiling. She had never worn makeup before and this transformation, this mask would finally help her blend in. Feel acceptable.

Frankie glanced at her wristwatch. "Oh, no. I think we should head back or else your date will be wondering where you've run off to."

Mac looked at Frankie through the mirror. "What time is it now?"

"Quarter to seven," Donovan announced.

Frankie patted her tush. "Time to book it outta here, kiddo."

☙❧

Her high heels sunk deep into the sand and with every step she kicked up the grainy bits as she walked from Frankie's house to hers. At the shop Machiko had preferred the sensible pair of flats but Donovan had insisted she try on a pair of black T-strap heels from a new designer line. She had refused but after much convincing she had fallen in love with them for their fit and comfortability.

She tried to blow a wisp of stray hair off her face without any success. Giving up, she lifted her chin to shake the strands back in place and that's when she caught sight of her visitor. Even from the distance she recognized Caleb sitting on her porch swing dressed to the nines in a charcoal suit and a crisp black shirt to match. His arm was draped leisurely over the back of the seat and he looked like he didn't have a care in the world.

When he spotted her, he practically hopped off the swing, straightening up as he waited for her. While she took the seven steps up, his eyes raked boldly over her, causing her heart to flutter wildly in her breast.

"You're a goddess," he breathed.

Pleased by his comment, heat rushed to her cheeks and she smiled, but did not answer. It took several seconds for the compliment to sink in. She met his steady gaze and a vaguely sensuous light passed between them.

Silence rolled on. *Tick. Tick. Tick.*

Caleb cleared his throat and the heavy air of sexual attraction evaporated. "I didn't realize eight on the dot would be translated to eight forty-five Mac time."

"Frankie drove." Her response seemed to amuse him.

"Well that explains everything. You're lucky to be alive." He held out his arm to her. "Shall we? I'm sure my sister won't be too upset that we're going to be fashionably late. After all, it's L.A. and no one ever shows up on time."

In spite of herself, she laughed and took his arm. "By the way, nice haircut. So, you aren't growing it out?"

He shook his head. "Nope. I wanted you to feel guilty every time you look at my sexy, shiny bald head."

He wiggled his eyebrows and they both burst out laughing, sharing in on their very own secret.

Machiko had never laughed so hard in her life, her stomach constricted in pain and she tried to control her laughter. Her eyes roved over his face and she gave him a sober look as she spoke, "If it's any consolation, I think you've never looked more handsome."

His laugh broke off and his dark eyes pierced the distance between them. She licked her parched lips and his smoldering eyes froze on her mouth. That longing gaze set her body on fire with his intensity and she lowered her lashes to conceal her own desires.

Caleb reached out and caught her hand in his. His unexpected gesture made her conscious of the undeniable magnetism building between them.

Noisy chattering, clinking glasses, and the steady vibrations of techno music blared through the open door that led into a trendy brick building that housed the designer clothing boutique on Rodeo Drive. Caleb could see how uncomfortable Mac appeared by the way her eyes darted around the parameters while they waited to be checked off the guest list.

He wondered if pressuring her to go with him had been the right decision. From what he knew of her, she had social anxieties and he hoped to help her overcome her fears. Maybe get her to be more comfortable and less timid about meeting and making new friends.

"Your name sir?" The brawny bouncer directed his question with a stoic face while holding a clipboard in his hand.

"Caleb Holden and guest," He answered, his fingers weaving with Mac's. He gave her hand a light squeeze to remind her she wasn't alone.

He couldn't help feeling like one lucky sonofabitch. She really looked like a goddess tonight in that pearl chiffon gown with a twisted, one-shoulder Grecian-style cut, an empire waist, and draped fabric flowing in layers down to her calves. The dress could have been custom made for her and fully enhanced her silken skin.

Every time he snuck a peek her way he could feel a tingling sensation running down his spine, could imagine seeing her standing naked before him, casting a spell with those soulful eyes. Memories crashed his thoughts of the morning spent with her in his arms. He could almost smell her womanly scent; almost feel the wet pulse of satisfaction that washed through her all over again.

His thighs barely touched hers yet he couldn't fight his body's reaction to the beautiful woman beside him. He tried to think of the most unsavory mental images to counteract the sudden swelling in his trousers. Caleb couldn't wait to get inside and partake of the alcoholic beverages to help take the bite off of his lustful cravings.

Gemma ran to the door and squealed, "Oh my God! I didn't think I had invited Lex Luthor to my show."

He'd never been more relieved to see a familiar face in his life. Caleb let go of Mac and gave his sister a crushing hug. "Sorry I'm late. I had to make sure I was nice and polished."

He noticed Gemma's amused look as she appraised his newly bald head. "Um, any shinier and we won't need lights in there. Glad you've decided to come support your only sibling. You basically missed the unveiling, which was the most important part of the night. But hey, you came just in time for the free food and booze." Gemma quipped.

"I'll make it up to you. Promise."

She gave him an exaggerated wink. "In that case, hope you have enough in your bank account because I've got more than a dozen ways you can make it up to me." An eyebrow rose in interest as she eyed his companion. "Now, who's the lovely guest accompanying you tonight?"

He grinned as his sister's protectiveness showed through. "Mac Barrett, this is my wonderfully talented younger sister Gemma Holden."

"Nice to meet you." The women shook hands and he could feel the awkward undercurrent sizzling around them.

A courteous smile curved her mouth. "Let's introduce you around." She looped her arm through Mac's arm and led her in as he followed the women.

Caleb didn't get very far when several acquaintances stopped to greet him. He tried to seek Mac out through the bevy of guests but realized his sister had just hijacked his date. If he knew Gemma, she would be doing an in-depth interrogation that would test Mac's endurance and patience.

He felt a light pressure on his back and turned to discover his ex-girlfriend, a seductive pout on her lips. Her British accent thick with surprise, "Wow, I haven't seen you in a few weeks and those beautiful dark locks are missing." She slid her arms around his neck and gave him an intimate kiss.

"Jordan. I thought it was time for a change." He untangled out of her embrace and wiped the lipstick smudge off his lips.

"I was asking your sister why you didn't invite me to join you tonight."

"Well, I knew Gemma had planned on inviting you." A server stopped by briefly and he took two glasses of champagne, handing her one.

He practically drained the contents in one drink.

Jordan placed a perfectly manicured hand on his chest. "I've missed you. The bed has been cold without you keeping me warm."

"We've discussed this, Jordie. We tried before and it didn't work out. I respect your friendship too much and I think we both need to move on." He lowered his voice. "It's better this way. It's different now."

She pulled her hand away, hurt flitted across her eyes and he knew she'd forgive him some day. For now, if he didn't nip it in the bud, she would try to seduce him into her bed again. He wasn't the same man from a few weeks ago. He didn't feel the spark of desire in her presence, not like with Mac. *Where was she, anyway?* His eyes made a full sweep of the place and she was nowhere to be found.

"I see." Jordan straightened her spine, her tone becoming chilly. "I'm going to go check out Gemma's collection before everyone snatches them up. It was good seeing you." She didn't meet his eyes again.

He opened his mouth to respond when a blur of white chiffon whizzed past him. He grabbed Mac's wrist, "Whoa. Where's the fire?"

Her eyes were brimming with tears, anger brewing in their depths.

"I'm going home. I knew it was a bad idea to come." She yanked her hand free and took off.

"Wait, Mac. What happened?" His head whipped around and he saw the guilty expression, as clear as day, written all over his sister's face.

What had Gemma done?

Chapter Seven

Machiko rubbed her dry eyes and felt the strain from long hours of strenuous focus and sleep deprivation. Had it been a week since Machiko left the party and locked herself in the beach house, immersing herself in her paintings?

She stared blankly at the canvas. The woman's sorrowful expression reached out to her, one delicate hand barely covering her breasts and the other sheltering her mound. She couldn't look away, was drawn to this painting, loved the contrast of the colors. This was a new technique for her and she focused on using varying shades of black and gray to give the woman a dreamlike effect. The dark shades of red and orange were used to emphasize the fire blazing around the woman's body like a cloak.

Her fingers tingled, numb and aching from the grip she had on the paintbrush. Too tired to concentrate, the brush slipped out of her grasp and paint splattered and the object rolled across the hardwood floor.

No matter how much effort she put into her paintings, she couldn't push the images of Caleb away. The hurt and humiliation still lingered with her. She was no good for anyone, especially for him. How could she tell him the truth when she still couldn't deal with it herself?

Damn Caleb for making her believe that she could be different, be someone else!

The room started to spin and she took a few deep breaths to steady herself. Machiko hadn't left the house in days. Her eyes burned and she felt the strain of not taking care of herself. Fatigue was catching up with her but she didn't give a damn. She wanted to lock herself in where she didn't have to deal with anything or anyone.

There was no pretending now. She could be herself here.

The answering machine beeped from somewhere in the living room and she knew the voicemail box was full. She hadn't answered any of Caleb's calls or listened to his messages. She hadn't opened the door for him even when he had pounded incessantly to gain her attention. The man went as far as sleeping on her swing, but in the end he had given up.

Just as she suspected.

Oh, he could crawl under a girl's skin! A real pain in the ass and he liked pushing her buttons. She didn't need him coming around anyway. She didn't miss his stupid jokes or hoity-toity manners. She certainly didn't miss his company or his presence. Good riddance. She didn't need to make any more small talk because she was all by her lonesome.

And now, there was silence.

Complete and utter silence.

Just her and the discarded gown still bunched on the floor in the corner.

Sometime during the morning she had grown tired of the easel and propped the canvas on a large paint can against the wall. She tried to stand but her body didn't want to work with her. Her muscles had cramped up from hours of squatting on the floor. She had been in the zone and nothing would have pulled her away from the painting. Her aching body made it difficult to maneuver as she stepped back to view her latest creation.

She felt a warm glow of accomplishment flow through her.

The pain was well worth the effort.

Machiko hadn't bothered securing any newspapers around her work area and streaks of color covered the wall around the painting like a halo. *It's an artist's imprint*, her weary mind offered. She yawned, deciding to resume painting after she got some shuteye. Sleep sounded heavenly and a plush, comfy bed was enough to persuade her to leave the studio.

Machiko pushed back the tangled pieces of hair from her face. Her stomach growled and a dull pain followed. She scratched her itchy scalp. Had she eaten? She couldn't remember the last time she had a decent meal, or slept for that matter. She let out another yawn. Sleep would help with the sudden memory lapse. Feeling dazed, she staggered through the room without caring for the hurricane of a mess she had left in her wake.

❦

"I'm so sorry, Caleb. I really don't know what happened last week." Gemma's distraught face garnered a small amount of sympathy from him.

"What the hell made her take off like that? What did you say to her?" His frown deepened with every question.

"One moment I was introducing her to some friends of mine and the next she looked as if she'd seen a ghost. When I asked her what was wrong she was already halfway out the door."

He weighed the words in his head as he paced across his living room. Out of habit he ran his hand over his hair and realized he had deliberately kept it clean-shaven since the day Mac had given her trust to him. What could have made her run away from him? Had he done something wrong?

His eyes widened, suddenly the answer hit him like a bullet train. "Shit. I think I figured it out," he mumbled more for his own sake.

Gemma crossed her arms and leaned back against the bar counter. "I hope you would shed some light on it for me, because for the life of me, I don't believe it's my fault."

He stopped pacing and looked her square in the eyes. "I think she saw Jordie kissing me."

"Serious? Do you think that's what happened? God, you're such a dog!" Gemma gave him a dirty look.

His brows crease together. "C'mon, give me some more credit than that."

"You're absolutely right. However, your track record on dating hasn't been the most..."

He snapped, "I got it already." Caleb walked around to the back of the bar and grabbed a bottle of Glenfiddich. He flipped a glass over and poured some of the Scotch whisky in. "It's different this time." He didn't bother looking at her.

Gemma took a seat at the bar. "Really. How so?"

He tipped the slender, green bottle at Gemma and she nodded in response to his silent question. "Mac's a nice girl but I wouldn't want her to think I asked her to go with me and then make out with the first woman who approached me." He slid his glass over to her, grabbed another glass and poured himself one.

She grinned from ear-to-ear. "Somebody's got a crush." Gemma drained the liquid then blotted her lips daintily.

"Don't be absurd. We're just friends," he snorted. His sister had an overactive imagination at times and even her insinuations sounded ridiculous.

"She's gorgeous, that's for sure." Gemma grabbed the bottle and refilled their glasses.

"Isn't she?" Caleb stared into his drink as images of Mac flashed in his head. Beautiful creamy skin and a tight little body he'd like to get his hands on. He cleared his throat and quickly added, "I mean, she didn't look half bad the other night."

"Well, the woman had good taste in shoes, that's for sure." This time she took a sip of the drink as if she wanted to savor the taste. "I don't know how she scored a pair of my shoes but I was rather impressed. Come to think of it, I did send a handful of my early releases out to a few exclusive shops around town..."

"Enough about you."

Gemma stuck out her tongue and he shook his head at her.

There was no way in hell he had a crush on Mac. So maybe she was hot, but that didn't mean anything. Every time they had a conversation one of them would wind up pissed off. He was trying to be her friend. If others misconstrued his intentions, that was their own damn problem.

He couldn't seem to forget the last image he had of her and her reaction had stayed with him for days. Caleb downed his drink, recalling the painful expression on Mac's face. He could understand her feeling betrayed and humiliated if she had witnessed him kissing another girl. He was a dickhead.

Christ, he had told Mac to trust him and he had failed her.

"Gems, I really fucked up this time."

Her head bobbed up and down in agreement. "You're telling me." She gave him a sympathetic look and after a brief pause she asked, "So what are you going to do about it then?"

❦

"Wake up, Mac." Groggy and exhausted, she managed to open her eyes. Her eyelids drooped heavily but she blinked a few times until his handsome face came into focus.

"H-how did you get...get in here?" she mumbled through dry, cracked lips.

His worried frown transformed into an expression of relief and he expelled a short breath. Caleb held up a key. "Luc likes for me to have a spare in case of an emergency."

He helped pull her into a sitting position.

"Here, have some of this." He brought a glass to her lips and she sipped the cool liquid slowly at first then sucked down as much of the water as possible.

"Slow down, sweetie. There's plenty more where this came from."

In her delirious state she understood and complied. When she had satiated her need for fluids, he placed the glass on her nightstand. "Thank God I checked in on you. For all I knew, you could be rotting away in here." His teasing tone had an edge of seriousness.

"I can take care of myself," she croaked.

"Right. You can barely sit up on your own and you're telling me that I should just walk out and let you waste away?" A muscle flicked angrily at his jaw. "You're all skin and bones."

She tried pushing him away, but she didn't have the energy and collapsed back against him. "I hate you."

He stroked her hair tenderly. "No, you hate the fact that I'm right."

His words triggered a painful memory, breaking the dam that she had spent years trying to safeguard. A fat tear rolled down her cheek but she refused to give into the pain or the tears. Her bones ached with a hollowness that reverberated through her.

"Don't, Caleb," she choked out.

"Look. I don't want to upset you. At least eat some food I've brought over. But maybe you might want to take a shower first. "You smell ripe." He wrinkled his nose to prove his point, breaking the tension.

"Thanks for your honesty."

He laughed, his voice soothing when he spoke. "I'll help you to the bathroom and while you're showering I'll have the food hot and waiting for you."

Machiko pressed a finger to his lips. "Okay. Anything to get you to shut up. You're giving me a headache." Her lips twisted into a faint smile and he kissed her fingertips.

He got up off the bed. "I'll get the shower going and will put some towels in there."

When he was halfway across the room she blurted, "Caleb."

He stopped at the door, didn't turn around, simply waited.

"You were right." She swallowed hard before adding, "Don't read too much into it."

Caleb laughed and seemed to visibly relax. "You're welcome," he said over his shoulder before continuing on.

Twenty–five minutes passed and she still hadn't emerged. He tapped his fingers on the table waiting for Mac to come out. He hoped she hadn't slipped and fell. *Maybe she cracked her skull open and was bleeding to death on the floor.* Caleb didn't wait to delve into that thought and scooted out of the chair. He heard light footsteps and dropped back down, pretending to be fascinated with his diet soft drink.

"Oh. Out so soon?" The nonchalant question died on his lips.

Speechless, his eyes roamed over her figure. She was a vision standing before him. Her hair was still damp and the recent shower gave her cheeks a nice rosy color. His impatience dissolved at seeing her more rejuvenated, and sexy as hell in that outfit.

She had donned on a white tank top and a pair of cutoff camouflage cargos. She hadn't bothered wearing a bra and he could see the hardened nipples poking through the thin fabric. His shaft hardened in response to the illicit thoughts whirling inside. He'd give anything to spread her on the table and feast on those perfect nipples. Worship every inch of her silky skin. *Focus, Holden. Focus.*

He was thankful he was sitting down, his lower body hidden from view. Caleb mustered a lopsided smile through the lust-filled agony. She was killing him slowly.

She took a seat across from him. "I thought I'd spend a few extra minutes exfoliating since someone mentioned I smelled bad."

He chuckled as he made preparations to feed her. He piled a little of everything from the Chinese takeout onto her plate, then placed the heaping portion in front of her. He made friendly small talk as he watched her tear into the food, careful not to force the topic of the other night. Frankly, he wasn't ready to discuss Jordie. Not when they were getting along, finally making progress.

How the hell was he going to explain what happened without coming off as a prick? No, he'd wait to talk to her about this later.

He needed to change the topic before he slipped up.

"Say, I was wondering if I could have a look at your paintings." He gulped his drink while he observed her closely.

Mac stopped chewing, her hand holding the fork in mid-spear, her spine rigid. "They're not ready," she snapped.

"Why don't you want me to see them?"

"I don't like showing unfinished work. That's all." She made her statement and that sounded like the end of the subject.

Caleb couldn't help prying deeper. "What are you afraid of?"

Mac pushed the plate aside. "I think you need to leave."

"What? You're asking me to go because I asked you one simple question?"

"I'd like some time alone." Unspoken pain was alive and glowing in her eyes.

"You can't push me away forever. When are you going to get it into your thick skull I'm not going anywhere?"

She stood up. Her dark eyes became flat and unreadable as stone. "You're right. You're not going anywhere but I'll be leaving as soon as the summer's over."

Her words hit home. He had forgotten she wasn't from here. Why was he fighting so hard to be her friend when she was as fleeting as her emotions? Caleb pushed back his seat and got up. "Right."

He couldn't bear looking at her. The thought of her leaving never crossed his mind. She would be out of his life in a few short months, maybe forever. His chest grew heavy from the truth of the knowledge.

"Thanks for dinner." She dropped her eyes to the floor and crossed her arms, trying to avoid looking at him.

Caleb's hands balled into fists at his side. He didn't want to believe any of this. No, he wasn't going to let her control things.

She raised her eyes and he could see the confusion swimming inside.

That look told him all he needed to know.

"It's not over, Mac." His words were meant as both a threat and a promise.

Chapter Eight

"Excuse me." Machiko shielded her eyes and squinted up at the beautiful brunette with high cheekbones and a million dollar smile. From her bed in the sand, the woman looked like an Amazon princess impatiently waiting for an answer from her minion.

This morning she had gotten up early with the intention of starting her next painting, however, the sun and ocean had other plans for her.

She was lured outside to bathe in the warm morning rays and take advantage of the day before the summer passed her by. She had managed to settle back for some relaxation, had made a pillow out of her towel, and used the sand as her bed when she was disrupted by the distinct British accent.

"Sorry. I was wondering if you had seen the man who lives two houses down from you."

Feeling at a disadvantage from her angle, Machiko sat up to address the woman. "You're talking about Caleb?"

The brunette nodded. "Yes. Caleb Holden. Have you seen him?"

Machiko hadn't seen him in four days, not that she was

counting. Their conversation, still fresh on her mind, nagged at her conscience at the way she handled the situation. Her lips turned into a frown. He had commented about things not being over, yet disappeared under the radar without any signs of resurfacing.

She hated to admit she missed his company. Every time the swing creaked on her porch she thought of him. Those vibrant brown eyes, the rich sound of his voice. She ached to remember the times he made her laugh when she wasn't in the mood. No one had ever made her this comfortable. No one ever cared enough to.

"Well? Have you seen him?" The brunette pursed her lips in irritation. Her oversized sunglasses glinted from the reflection of the sun.

"No. I haven't seen him in a while."

She straightened up. "If you do, could you tell him Jordan came calling?" By the woman's unconscious pose, Machiko imagined there was years of modeling ingrained in her.

She tilted back her head. "If I see him."

Jordan gave her the once over. "You're new. Did you just move in?"

"I've been here for a few weeks. Just housesitting for the Delacroix for a little while."

"I see. Have you had the chance to visit with Caleb?"

Machiko shielded her eyes from the glare of the sun. "Once or twice."

"You know, he could be a real flirt. Watch out that you don't get your heart broken." The knowing smile on Jordan's face made her feel uneasy.

"Oh, don't worry. I'm just using him for the sex." Her eyes were steady on the woman who seemed to be unhappy with her response.

"Right. I'll be off then." She abruptly turned on her designer clad heels, kicking flecks of sand back at Machiko as she walked away.

She hadn't heard Frankie approach until her neighbor remarked dryly, "Looks like you've found a new friend in

Jordan Fenley."

She rubbed her face and tried to brush the sand off her eyelids. "Friendly Fenley." Machiko grinned.

"That she is." Frankie held out her hand and she took it as the woman helped pull her up. "I like the bit about the sex." Her laughter eased the tension from the awkward situation.

They walked toward Machiko's house. Her curiosity got the better of her. "What's her relation to Caleb?"

"Well, they were an item for a while. I don't know the specifics as to why they broke up, but they're still good friends from what I hear."

"She's beautiful."

"Beauty can be skin deep."

Machiko followed her through the house to the kitchen. "Something I should know?"

Frankie grabbed two Coronas from the fridge, flipped off the cap with the help of the edge of the counter and a strong hold, and handed Machiko one. "No more than what I know. So, kiddo, how's the progress?"

She took a long swallow of her drink, weighing her thoughts before speaking. "Almost complete."

Frankie's eyes lit up. "Have you decided to show at the gallery? I know Luc has been hounding you for an answer on the date."

"I'm not so sure I can do this. I thought I was ready, but a part of me feels torn."

"That's because you can't see things objectively. You need a fresh eye and an expert opinion." Frankie winked.

Machiko had spent so many years away from her craft that the more she painted the less she became confident of her abilities. Truth be told, she was scared. The thought of allowing the public to see her work made her feel vulnerable, as if she was stripped naked before them as they scrutinized her every flaw. She wasn't sure if the mask she had hidden behind would cover all the past mistakes.

Especially after the night at Gemma's shoe event.

Frankie was one of the few people she had ever trusted and

she fought the urge to tell her the truth. Her soul felt heavy with indecision. She needed to confide in someone.

Machiko spoke with caution, "If I were to tell you something..." She took another swig of her beer.

"You can tell me anything. I don't judge." Frankie reached out and patted her hand.

"This is something I've never talked about. It's been so long that it feels like it was a life belonging to someone else." Machiko took a deep breath and continued, "There are so many secrets that I've tried to hide but I can't do it anymore. I'm starting to suffocate and I need to face the truth."

"Here, here. There's no rush." Frankie's expression was filled with maternal tenderness.

Machiko couldn't believe she was about to bare her soul, finally open herself up. Was this the right thing to do? She didn't have the strength to keep the secret and she knew in her heart it was time to talk about it.

She gripped the bottle so tight her knuckles whitened. "I've lied about everything."

"What do you mean? Lied about what, dear?"

"Everything. About who I really am. Why I'm here."

Frankie's eyebrow quirked up. "I don't understand."

"Years ago, I was known as Hoshi Machiko Barrett-Kingston." She let the words sink in. After all these years the name still sounded foreign to her.

"That name sounds a bit familiar." A few seconds passed and Frankie's eyes suddenly widened, then narrowed as realization set in. "Oh, my God. Hoshi Kingston, the child artist. The three-year-old prodigy whose paintings were praised for your use of colors and precise technique? You virtually disappeared at thirteen-years-old, never to be heard of again."

Machiko nodded sadly. "Yes. One and the same." She could feel the painful lump form in her chest, blocking her breathing as the memories came hurtling back.

"You're a legend." Frankie raised a finger and polished off her beer in one long swallow. "Hell, I'm going to need more than one drink to get through this." Frankie took off for the bar and a few minutes later she came back with a bottle of Glenlivet and two glasses. She poured generous portions of the pale gold whisky into the glasses and held one out to Machiko.

"Go on, love."

She cradled the glass to her. The hollowness in her soul expanded at the thought of the repercussions from her actions. "I lied about the paintings and told the media my father had helped me produce them. I ruined his good name and destroyed his professional career. I tore apart my family in one fell swoop. All because I was selfish." She didn't feel the tears until a liquid drop hit her hand. A hand that was fisted so tight that her nails cut into her flesh.

"You weren't selfish. You were lost. Now drink up, dear." Frankie drained her glass and refilled another.

Sipping the whisky, Machiko tasted the subtle peatiness with its delicate, slightly fruity and vanilla flavor. Clean and well-balanced. She felt the warmth instantly heat up her belly and she closed her eyes to allow the alcohol to dull some of the pain.

"What happened after that?"

Machiko opened her eyes and her hands trembled. "I had a nervous breakdown. My parents checked me into a facility for treatment."

Frankie's eyes flashed angrily. "Their solution was a loony bin?"

"I don't blame my parents. It was their only choice at the time. The mental health retreat was not as bad as it sounds. I had all the medical care and assistance I needed."

"Christ, Mac. You were a child. What you needed was love and understanding. Maybe a good spanking, but you should never have had to be subjected to that."

"No, I don't want to look at it that way. I learned from the experience and I was able to start over. I could be anything I want without the dark shadow following me."

Frankie shook her head. "Reinventing yourself doesn't make up for the fact that the scars are still there. You've only pushed it back into the recesses of your mind and one day it's going come back in full force and kick you in the ass."

"I've spent my life burying that person and I'm going to make damn sure she stays buried."

Frankie placed a hand on Machiko's cheek. "And what if the girl inside resurfaced?"

The question hit her like a blow to the gut.

You know the answer, Machiko.

She couldn't breathe. Her head swam with all the fears that had seized her heart and a dizzy feeling of dread crept in. She remembered Caleb's gorgeous eyes, heard the whispered conversations, the condemnation and laughter. A vision of a girl lost alone in the corner soon morphed into brilliant colors splashed across an oversized canvas. The painting clearly materialized in her mind as she recalled that night.

The familiar painting was her teardrops on canvas hanging at the back of the store, a bold reminder of who she was. Still is. Her very last masterpiece still existed, the colors bleeding with torment and sorrow on the surface before her world became the darkest kind of hell.

Machiko had collided face-to-face with her past the night she had gone with Caleb to his sister's private event.

A tremble touched her lips as she looked Frankie in the eyes and said shakily, "The girl inside already did."

⚜

Machiko paced back and forth in front of Caleb's door, indecision gripping her conscience. She sucked in her breath and stopped to face the front door. What was she doing here? Why was she trying to make peace with someone who had abandoned her? She whirled around to make a hasty retreat when the front door jerked open.

"Why didn't you just ring the damned doorbell?"

She turned right back around and her heart squeezed at seeing his handsome face again.

"I forgot something." Her feeble mind conjured up the lie.

He pointed to the large, wrapped gift she was holding onto. "So what's that in your hand?"

What could she say? That she had missed him and was trying to win back his friendship? She had never needed to hold on to friends because she had never truly had one. Now she had Frankie and in a bizarre way, she had Caleb.

She pushed the gift at him. "A peace offering."

Caleb's frown transformed into a grin as he accepted the present. She jutted out her chin. "That's it."

"Wanna come in?" He pushed the door wider and moved aside.

Machiko hadn't intended on more than a brief exchange of words yet the coziness of his home beckoned. Her eyes returned to his face, the slightly crooked nose, the angular jaw, a few days growth of beard. Oh, she had noticed every part of him, from the way his muscles rippled under his t-shirt to the snug fit of his jeans. The electricity sparked and she knew coming was a big mistake.

"I can't. I've got work to do."

"I'm sure it can wait for a few minutes," his throaty voice persuaded.

She bit her lower lip to keep from throwing herself at him. God, she missed his lips. Missed the feel of his tongue and the way he made her feel. How could a man radiate such intensity and not know it?

"Only a few minutes," she breathed.

He reached out and grabbed her hand, pulling her inside, as if he was afraid she'd run.

Once in the living room, Machiko withdrew her hand quickly, afraid of her body's reaction.

"Have a seat." He pushed her gently onto the sofa and plopped down on the coffee table across from her.

"May I?" Caleb eagerly eyed the gift in his hand.

"I was hoping you'd want to wait to do it later..." her answer trailed off when he ripped into the wrapping paper.

His hands froze in mid-tear, his body taut as he stared at the visible part of the painting. Caleb didn't speak and finished tearing the rest of the wrapping off. He held the painting up with both hands, admiring the gift.

Caleb was utterly speechless. Surprised was not the word he had in mind. Fucking shocked was more like it. Not only had she managed to make the first move but she brought him this exquisite canvas that she called a peace offering. How could he rightfully accept something this valuable?

He couldn't reject the gift. Why would he want to? The painting was clearly a reflection of Machiko, and if this was a clue, he was willing to scrutinize it until he figured her out. Caleb stared at the overall image yet the woman's eyes captivated him, drowning him with its sorrow. Her sultry lips reminded him of the heated kisses he had shared with *her*.

Caleb carefully propped the painting against the lounge chair and turned to Machiko. "I don't know what to say."

"Look, I thought about what you said the last time we spoke and you're right." She laced her fingers together. "I shouldn't have made a fuss about not letting you see my work. Now you own an original." Her attempt at a smile softened the seriousness of her face.

Caleb didn't know what was worse, being haunted by the painting he was just given or by the woman who gave it to him. Her eyes were dark and unfathomable, leaving him breathless. He reached out and touched her trembling lips with his finger. "Your painting moved me."

She opened her mouth and he shook his head. "Sensual, breathtaking, rich with emotion…"

"Passionate," she whispered against his finger.

His cock swelled to life and he had the urge to taste those hot, sumptuous lips. He swallowed hard. "Passionate? I was going to say naïve."

She pulled away from him, her eyes still glowing from their interaction. His lips curled into a smile.

"You think I'm naïve? I paint what I know and what I feel. I've never been dishonest in what I chose to portray," her voice raised a notch.

He grinned at her defensiveness and he could see the effect it was causing. "You're barely more than a child. I don't think you've fully grasped the concept of being a woman. Let alone know what the meaning of passion is. It's obvious by your interaction with people that you've lived in a bubble for so long you could barely keep up a civilized conversation with me when we first met."

"I resent that statement. I've had to grow up fast so don't tell me what I know and don't know." She pushed herself to a standing position. "I'm not some virgin who hasn't experienced dirty, torrid sex!"

Caleb stood up, clearly towering over her, and looked down into her pretty face. "Torrid sex? You sound like a virgin to me."

"You pompous ass. I can't believe I would want to have you as a friend." She started to leave and he grabbed her wrist, swinging her around to face him.

She licked her lush lips and that was enough to drive him over the edge. Their heated conversations always lit a fire in him, especially how damn desirable she looked in that halter top and plaid mini-skirt.

He captured her lips with a hunger, his kiss cruel and rough as he took what he wanted, needed. He had to have more of her. His tongue traced the soft fullness of her lips and when she gasped, raising herself to meet his kiss, he plunged his tongue inside and explored the recesses of her mouth. Velvet, sweet, lovely.

She tasted like a summer dessert, so light and creamy. He had an endless need to kiss her until she grew limp in his arms, panting for more. He pulled her hard against him and his lips moved across her jawline, down her neck, her shoulders. Her hardened nipples rubbed tight against his chest and his hands slid to her firm, round ass. He grabbed the solid flesh beneath her skirt and pressed her tight against his erection.

He could hear her heart beating hard against her breast and the sound invigorated him. Her arousal became his fire, quickly consuming him by her response. Caleb dropped to his knees and pushed up her skirt. His mouth covered her mound and she moaned as he ran his tongue across the laced fabric.

He inhaled her scent. She smelled of cherry blossoms in bloom and he suddenly felt the need to teach her a lesson they'd both enjoy. He flicked his tongue against her clit and she gripped his shoulders. His mouth and lips praised her femininity with every kiss, every sweep of his tongue. Her moans grew, her breathing increased and the more she reacted to him the more he wanted to please her.

So wrapped up in pleasuring her, he was stunned when she pushed him away. Machiko pulled down her skirt and he watched the horror splash across her face.

"This can't happen. This shouldn't happen." She stepped away and continued to ramble, "I thought I wanted it but now I don't want it anymore. I don't want you anymore."

"Wait, Mac. Let's talk about this." He got up but she was halfway out the door.

She stopped, tightfisted. She said in a stricken voice, "It's all a game. You don't want me. You never will." With those words she slammed the door and he could only look on, not knowing how to respond.

Was everything she said the truth? Did he only see her as a game, a puzzle to unravel? Caleb dropped his head and he caught sight of the painting from out of the corner of his eyes. He couldn't seem to shake her image. Those gentle almond eyes, the way she crinkled her nose when she didn't like his joke, the way she consumed him every time she was with him.

In that moment, he realized he had to have her.

Chapter Nine

"**W**ow." Gemma's mouth hung agape. "Just wow." She stared at the painting with a critical eye.

Caleb rubbed his jaw, aware of the two days growth of stubble. "The details are incredible, so graceful and…"

"*Hot*!" She giggled. "Sorry. I've never seen a painting that could make me blush just by looking at it."

He laughed at his sister's candor. How could he tell her he had obsessed over the painting since Mac had given it to him? There was something distinctly familiar about her painting technique but he couldn't quite put a finger on it.

The analytical side of him wanted to dissect the meaning of every brush stroke, uncover the secret code hidden within. How could a face so innocent bear such internal scars? She was this enigma who only offered him a glimpse of what she wanted him to see. It was like dangling a carrot in front of a horse and spurred him to want to learn more about her. No, he needed to know what she was all about.

Machiko took his breath away. Her eyes always begged him to save her soul, but from what? He focused on the painting that now replaced his Chagall. The manifestation of Mac was an image of purity enveloped within the cocoon of a fiery hell. The message was haunting and knotted him up inside. Caleb had always thought that art was much like writing. A writer often wrote down his innermost fears but added a pinch of embellishment to draw interest.

In this case, a painter portrays her deepest fears, laid out all her insecurities for the world to see without having to embellish. Art was vulnerable and those who could read the message would gain insight into the artist's soul. Perhaps that was where his fascination for collecting art stemmed from. It was more than cracking the code. Reading paintings was like a drug he never wanted to kick. Somehow, he knew without a doubt that Mac understood him more than anyone else he had ever known.

Her ability to read his Chagall the first day she came to his house had proved to him that they spoke the same language, a subliminal connection that few would ever understand. That's why he couldn't let it go. He wouldn't let her shut him out without taking a bite out of the forbidden apple.

"I can't believe I'm about to ask you for a favor."

"A favor? That's the first." Gemma's amused look made him want to retract what he had just said. "Let's see, does it concern a particular neighbor who has gotten you so wound up that you would voluntarily go bald to stay in her good graces?"

"I knew it was a mistake." He palmed his bald head.

"C'mon. I've never seen you so bipolar. Even when you were dating Jordan, you've always been calm, cool and collected. Now, I'm afraid your temperament is like a crap shoot of surprises."

Caleb rubbed his bare head again. "I wonder if the hospital traded out my baby brother for you."

"You know I absolutely adore you!" She pinched his cheek and laughed. "Clock's ticking, so let's get down to the nitty gritty. What can I possibly do to help my big brother out?"

He nodded, taking a seat on the leather sofa. Gemma dropped down beside him.

How could something so simple feel so complicated? He

settled back against the plush cushion and gazed up at the painting for the umpteenth time. He was torn between laughter and madness.

There had to be a plausible explanation. Maybe she used some sort of black arts to fuck with him because Mac was driving his imagination and sex drive into sensory overload. He swore if he focused hard enough he could almost believe the flames leapt to life, licking seductively around the exquisite figure.

Caleb twisted in his seat to face his sister, eye-to-eye. "What I wanted to ask you...well, frankly, I think Mac needs a friend. Not just any kind. I think she needs a girl friend."

Gemma smacked him on the forehead. "Whoa. I never signed up to be a lipstick lesbian."

"Jeez, Gemma! That's not what I'm saying. If you hadn't gathered, Mac lacks a kind of feminine etiquette. It might be nice for her to have a friend that's a girl!"

"All right, all right. I'll see what I can do. You want the 4-1-1 on the Mysterious Mac. If you ask me, she's a bit of an oddball but, hey, if that's your thing..."

"I didn't ask."

She crossed her arms and scowled. "Fine. Whatever. Just for the record, I hate befriending your girlfriends because in the end, I'm the one who gets shafted. They all drop me like a bad habit because they can't stand the sight of you and I'm suddenly guilty by association. For once, can't you just keep one? Please?"

Caleb draped an arm around his sister, pulling her close to him. "Poor baby. I suppose your kind deeds will involve me breaking out my checkbook again."

Her pout turned into an infectious grin. "You bet your sweet ass."

⚜

Steam rose up from the bath in soft curls, filling the room with a scent of freshly cut roses and springtime. Machiko leaned her head back against the ceramic tub and settled deeper into the warmth of the soothing liquid. She hadn't had a moment's peace since meeting Caleb. She hated the fact that his image would force its way into her brain at any given time. The man had the ability to trigger her lust mechanism whenever he was near.

Compared to other women, she was probably considered a little inexperienced in the lovemaking department. Her lips curled in disgust. She could count the number of lovers on one hand. *How pathetic!* No wonder she was so intrigued by Caleb. He oozed sexual confidence.

Then there's his athletic physique, whenever he devoured her with his hungry eyes, she believed he had the expertise to break out any Kama Sutra pose in the book with acrobatic skill.

She shivered just thinking about him. *How could someone so annoying be so scrumptious?*

Machiko wished she had given into him the other day instead of scuttling off like some prudish schoolgirl. She wouldn't be surprised if he avoided her like the plague. Who could blame him?

She sank deeper into the water until her head was completely submerged. She held her breath, trying to zero in on that safe space in her memory. Why couldn't she find the comfort zone? What was happening to her that she could no longer control anything in her life? The peace never came and she re-emerged, letting out her breath and sucking in a lungful of air as if everything was polluted around her and there wasn't enough oxygen to take in.

Damn Caleb Holden and his efforts to charm her!

She didn't want to be charmed. She wanted to be left alone. Now that was a lie even to her own ears. She had never craved company more than she craved Caleb. How had he managed to break through the shell she constructed and get away with it?

"Naïve! I am not." She seethed at the memory. "How dare he tell me I lacked passion? A child? Not even."

A rush of sensual confusion tickled across her body and she touched her lips, summoning impure thoughts. His kisses were like an electromagnetic field that could wipe all cognitive thoughts from her head. The man was dangerous and it wasn't the kind that left bloodshed. His solid body and those damn sexy tattoos had made her wet without him even trying to seduce her.

Hell, Caleb was the kind of man that could deflower a virgin without even touching her. She had firsthand knowledge of his mouth and hand techniques to know he was the most wicked kind of evil. A shiver raced through her and her pussy throbbed with need for satisfaction.

She closed her eyes and the phantom materialized. His skin glistening, his dragon's tattoo stirring to life. A hand glided across her face, down her neck to cup a breast, pinching a nipple to a hardened peak. Her other hand slid across the hollow between her breasts, lower to her belly and rested over her aching sex.

Her fingers brushed across soft curls and over the pulsing cleft, quickly dipping inside. Hot, wet, and ready. She parted her tender folds and ran her fingers across the delicate skin, trembling as she circled the flesh around her clit. She felt the electric surge tingling on her skin, could almost feel him touching her there.

She pushed a finger inside her heat, then another, moving in and out with slow deliberation. With every action she felt his attentions, saw his face, took pleasure from his touch. With every surge of delight that coursed through her, she came closer to the warmth of the light. She remembered how his lips tasted next to hers, the way he smelled of pure masculinity and ocean water, the way his own hands felt on her the morning he had thought she was drowning.

Her head swam with luscious visions as her fingers moved faster, rubbing, pinching, plunging inside, until her breathing quickened, her body arched, her thighs tensed as she crept closer to the edge.

The tension mounted, bursting like sprinkles of magic through her body and she shuddered, her body twisted into a spiral of heat that left her temporarily satiated and weak. Empty. Alone. Unfulfilled.

Caleb rang the doorbell with the consistency of a jackhammer without garnering any response. He let out an irritated breath and banged on the door, receiving the same results. No answer. *Where the hell was she?*

Mac had disconnected the phone and there was no way of contacting her. The crazy fool didn't even own a cell phone. He made a mental note to get her one tomorrow. As for tonight, he looked down at his watch, it was exactly seventy-two hours and thirty-nine seconds since she walked out of his house after he had unsuccessfully tried to make love to her. His frown deepened.

He hoped to God he wouldn't find her in the same state he had the first time around. He really didn't want to resort to using the spare key, but he had no choice in the matter. Wasn't it Luc that had asked him to keep an eye on her? This, technically, was honoring his friend's wishes and if anything were to happen to Mac... No, he wasn't going to think about it. If nothing was wrong he was going to do the honor of killing her himself. A half-smile touched his lips.

Caleb cracked his knuckles. He hated that she had tacked up a large impermeable, makeshift curtain to prevent anyone from looking into her studio. Even if the lights were on inside there was no chance of finding out. That really pissed him off. She could be unconscious on the floor, or any number of horrible things, but he was quick to stop himself from going there.

He took a deep breath to calm his current disposition. After a brief check of the parameters to make sure no one was looking, he walked over to the edge of the porch to the wooden carving of the laughing Buddha with his hands outstretched over his head, holding a hefty gold piece. Caleb reached into the statue's mouth and pulled out the key.

Music assaulted him upon entry as Nine Inch Nails' *Closer* blared from the Bose surround system. *Damn soundproof home!* He rushed through the living room, tripping over loose clothes and empty wine bottles. The smell of cinnamon and rose candles wafted through the room, filling his nostrils as he headed in the direction of the music. He skidded to a stop right outside the door leading to the art studio. "Well, I'll be—," he sucked in his breath, shaking from something entirely other than anger and dread.

Moonlight streamed through the panels of the overhead ceiling windows, spilling across Mac's body to reveal vivid colors of fresh paint splattered across her arms, torso, and the length of her thighs in an asymmetrical pattern. Her body now stained by her craft held a captivating allure that reminded him of her erotic painting. Detailed, fluid...so naïve.

Caleb couldn't drag his eyes from her picturesque innocence. A Waterhouse painting with golden skin beneath pin-straight, onyx hair and lucid dark eyes that conveyed a childlike eagerness while remaining emotionally guarded. A kitten caught in a storm.

His eyes darted around the room, taking in all the variations of canvases in different stages of completion. His adrenaline rush had tapered off and now he was cloaked in a different kind of energy that seized his entire being.

"Caleb. What are you doing here?"

He could see her lips move but couldn't hear a word of what she was saying over the blast of sound. Mesmerized for a few seconds by the allure of those lush lips, he snapped out of the haze and walked over to the high tech CD player, lowering the volume. He turned back to face her, unable to tear his eyes from her.

His chest tightened when she licked her lips, so subtle, yet such a sensual act.

How can she not know her own power?

"Wh...what are you doing here?" Her lips quivered as she spoke.

His voice was gruff, thick with lust when he was able to speak. "Luc tried calling you and was worried when the phone wouldn't work. He asked me to check in, but there was no way of getting a hold of you."

She blinked, her gaze never wavering. "I'm fine, you can go!"

"I wanted to thank you for the painting."

"You could have left me a note," she responded coolly.

He shifted uncomfortably. "I didn't like how the conversation ended."

"Why are you really here?" Her voice grew firmer.

He spat out, "I wanted to see you."

She smiled then, a vixen's wicked smile. "Perhaps you're more interested in collecting my paintings than in checking on my well-being."

He bent his head slightly forward, smiling back with the same cruel twist. "Perhaps you're right. A collector always wants to be the first to see all the goods."

"Are you mocking me, Caleb?"

"Clearly, it lacks real passion and emotions. It only possesses an *illusion* of those things. You manage to isolate them within the eyes and lips of the image, to draw the audience away from the rest of the painting. True passion emanates from the entire piece as a whole, not selectively."

"Do you paint, Caleb? Surely you don't or you would understand that my work radiates passion, seduction, eroticism. All those things that I know of."

His eyes swept over her body, her face. "Really? You know of all those things and are able to apply those emotions? I don't believe it. A woman who truly knew passion wouldn't have run out the way you did."

Her eyes flashed with unspoken anger, then simmered to a painful glare and he realized he may have crossed the line.

"I'm not going to defend myself to you. I think you're more frightened that I may be more woman than you have ever had, can ever handle."

Her words, her smug expression, her fucking exotic beauty messed with his head. Maybe there was some to truth to her words that he didn't want to hear. Caleb lashed out, "You speak of passion and pleasure in your paintings, but I don't believe you understand the meaning of sensuality, Machiko."

His words had spurred some life within her when her body language changed. Mac's eyes sparked with a fire he hadn't noticed before. Her gaze reminded him of a girl turned fierce warrior as she straightened her shoulders, ready to do battle.

"You act as if you can read my soul, the inner workings of me," her hands moved expressively with every word. "You don't think I know what passion is? Passion flows through my veins and with every stroke of my brush I feel desire, heartache, cravings so deep it haunts my nights and I stay awake to fulfill their wishes…"

Her heated response ignited a strong desire to claim her, a need to taste her, show her what the real meaning of passion was about. What can a girl-woman know about lust and eroticism when she spent most of her youth running?

He watched her nostrils flair, her breasts rising and falling with every breath and something snapped inside. All sanity escaped him. Without missing a beat, he took several long strides to cross the room. Caleb didn't allow her time to react or respond. He reached out and cupped her face, encircling her waist with his free hand as he dragged her body hard against him to capture her lips.

He gave her a hungry kiss, plunging his tongue into her mouth as he explored the exquisite velvet depths. Her response startled him as she returned the exploration with a quiet, yet fierce gentleness, like a flower slowly learning to bloom. His stomach clenched with an odd awareness that gave him a momentary pause.

Tonight, Caleb decided he would educate Machiko on the fine art of sensuality.

Chapter Ten

*R*apture soared, spinning a swathe of silky lust around her soul. Machiko had spent seconds, hours, days dreaming of this moment, dreaming of Caleb's kisses. And now, the wait was over.

His grasp was solid, virile as he crushed her close. His tongue conquering her resistance, mastering every stroke as he dueled and challenged her. She wrapped her arms around his neck, rising on tip-toes to meet him with a hunger that burned for him, yearned for him. She couldn't get enough of his sweet kisses and intensity radiated between them, could have easily melted the Antarctic.

He broke away to kiss the corner of her mouth, nipping, biting gently across her jaw line and settled at the base of her neck. His tongue continued the torturous descent while his hands thoroughly explored her. His fingertips glided across her skin and she felt the goose pimples follow his lead.

Her heart danced with excitement as she allowed herself to feel the rippling muscles. Following the smooth lines of every curve and dip, every flex and fold of his bicep, forearm. She was so caught up in her exploration that when he cupped her breast beneath the fabric of her top she gasped, trembling from the suddenness of his action. He tweaked, twisted, pinched a nipple which produced a soft groan from her lips. Her sex pulsated, ravenous for his touch.

Warmth spread like a river of sinful cravings, grasping for more, for something entirely unobtainable. Her pulse quickened, her heart thumped erratically when he bent his head to capture a hard pebble between his teeth. He squeezed the heavy breast, teasing and nipping at the swollen nipple through the fabric.

A delightful shiver of wanting ran through her and she clutched at his shirt. When he shifted, she didn't wait, yanking the fabric up and over his head before discarding it on the floor. He didn't seem to mind her impatience and returned the favor by helping her dispose of her own tank top.

She watched as a smile died on his lips when he gazed at her without her shirt on. Vulnerability set in and she had the urge to cover her breasts. As if he could read her mind, he leaned in closer to recapture her lips. His kiss was gentle, his hands kind, as he explored her mouth, sucking her lower lip, running his tongue along the swollen flesh.

Caleb gripped her bottom, pressing her against him, his free hand easing her up and she wrapped her legs around his waist. He took two steps forward and stabilized her before reaching out to rip the thick fabric off the wall. Moonlight flooded the room in rows of peekaboo spots across the hardwood floor. He pressed her back against the windowpane and she sucked in her breath, feeling the cold permeate her to the core.

Caleb's deep throaty laughter made her eyes shoot up to his face and she shivered, not from the bitter cold but from the magnificence of his features. The moonlight bathed his face in softness, yet the harsh planes of his jaw and cheekbones gave him a devilish, yet angelic look.

His eyes glowed like sprinkles of cinnamon across warm toffee and she thought for a nanosecond she could see through his soul. Could feel his heartbeat calling for her. She gravitated to him, not caring for the reasons why but she knew that whatever happened tonight, this was meant to be.

"Kiss me," she commanded and his mouth covered hers hungrily. Devouring her as if she was his last meal before an execution.

She ground herself against his hardness and he groaned. She let her body tell him what she wanted, what she needed from him. His kiss deepened, punished, bruised her lips. Spirals of ecstasy rushed through her and he pulled back just enough to gaze into her eyes.

"There's no running now."

She asked in a raspy voice, "Where would I go if not here with you?"

He pushed up her torn jean skirt. His eyes lingered on her choice of panties. "Jesus Christ, Mac," he breathed huskily.

His eyes smoldered with fire as he reached for her sheer material and peeled it off of her. He held the strip of lace in between his fingers and a mischievous grin formed. Caleb grabbed her wrist and wrapped the stretchy fabric around it.

"What are you doing?" She breathed between parted lips.

He didn't answer and simply reached for the other wrist to create temporary handcuffs. Her emotions whirled as he roused her pleasure just from witnessing the naughty glint in his eyes.

Caleb brushed his lips against hers to distract her attentions while he glided her hands up over her head. His lips inched its way to her ear. He whispered softly, "You must do as I say. If you move, I will walk away and leave you bound and wanting. Do you understand?"

She could feel the moisture between her thighs just by listening to the sound of that sexy timbre. Pleasure radiated outward at the subtle, delectable hint of a threat, a promise, and the absolutely erotic idea. She swallowed hard, her senses alert, her body screaming to be compromised by his kind of torment.

Machiko nodded in understanding.

"Good girl." He kissed her temple, sliding to his knees as if he was worshipping her.

His hands caressed her thighs and when he had a glimpse of her most private of parts, he seemed to be frozen in place. She could hear his shallow breathing and anticipation burned in the pit of her stomach. She trembled as he parted her thighs wider for a better look. Before she could react, his mouth covered her sex, his tongue explored the tender folds, his hands worked alongside his gentle movements in an exquisite way.

Tension inched through her, coiling tight as she arched her back, her arms aching to be free to touch him. She hissed when her shoulders touched the cold glass and could feel his deep sigh escape him. Still, he wouldn't let up, his mouth did wondrous things that made her senses reel as if short-circuited. He nipped, bit, and teased her sensitive flesh until she was in a lustful frenzy. He pinched her clit and she could not longer control herself. She lifted her hips and ground herself against his mouth, needing more and he gave as much as she demanded.

"Please," she begged hoarsely.

He gave her one quick lick and straightened up. "Not yet, my sweet. We're just beginning."

Her body felt betrayed, throbbing with the need to come. "I hate you."

"You'll thank me later." He straightened up and her heart jerked when he scooped her up. He took a few steps, must not have seen her small rows of paint cans, and kicked the contents all over the floor.

"Fuck. Sorry about the mess," he mumbled, then his dark expression transformed into something she didn't like.

"I've always had the urge to paint."

Her eyes widened when the light bulb clicked on. "Oh, no."

"Oh, yes."

She squealed when he dropped down to his knees and laid her over the bed of thick, wet paint. "You're crazy!"

She writhed and with every movement paint stained her body. The cool sensation seeped into her and she gave up, lying back against the cold liquid coating hard wood floors. Bound and helpless.

His laughter filled the room as he stripped out of the rest of his clothes. *Oh, my!* Her mouth watered at the sight of him wrapped in the moon's gentle halo. He was a fucking gladiator stripped of his armor and gloriously parading for her eyes alone. His cock hung rigid, smooth, so damn desirable. She licked her dry lips, dying to know how he tasted in her mouth. He was so gorgeous, too perfect for words.

She was fascinated by the pulse throbbing at his temple. One minute she was drooling over him and the next he covered her body with his massive form. He nuzzled her neck while quickly shedding her off the skirt, with its ragged hemline, before he settled on his side close to her.

Bright colors streaked across his golden skin and she bit back the desire to lick every inch of it. She knew the beautiful color was a result of years of water sports and outdoor activities. Unlike her Vampiress pale color which hardly ever experienced direct light, until she had moved here.

Caleb threaded his fingers through her hair and left an imprint of colors wherever he stroked. He leaned down and seized her lips, plunging his tongue between her parted lips. She kissed him back with the same gentle sensuality, bringing her hands up and around his neck. He chuckled against her mouth and she flicked her tongue out, swirling around the "O" of his mouth.

He reached back and wrenched off the temporary handcuffs. "What we're going to do doesn't require these."

He threw the scrap of lace aside. He cupped her cheek and smiled, could feel the wet smudge across her skin. She rubbed her face against his palm. "What shall you paint?"

"Well, let's see." He dipped two fingers into a puddle of paint and lightly traced a path over her skin.

She closed her eyes, feeling the smooth sensation as his fingers skimmed across her skin to form lines and shapes. She tried to make out what he was doing, her body remained taut, now a canvas for his fingers.

Every few minutes he would stop to kiss her lips and then continue his secret artistry. She giggled every time he faked a kiss just to shake it up a bit. A newfound euphoria and contentment filled her, stirring together a handful of emotions in one blazing big pot that had once been incredibly empty.

Caleb always made her feel beautiful. He had the ability to draw out the seductive woman inside. The woman she hid from the world, one in which she felt helpless. Alienated. She didn't want to be that woman any longer. She needed to be released but she wasn't sure how. Could Caleb set her free?

When his fingers glided across the circled path below her breasts, she trembled. His eyes bore into hers and she melted, liquefied into the pools of acrylics that bled across the floor. The full-bodied, yet gentle fumes had a unique smell of their own, not acidic, not pungent, but just enough tang to incite the lustful longings that spread between her thighs.

She was doused in the perfume of paint, his fingers her brush, his sensual technique her aphrodisiac. When he was finished he leaned back, the moon a spotlight on her body as he admired his handiwork.

"Wait right there. Don't move." He kissed her lips with a loud *SMACK* and rolled over to rummage into his jeans pocket. He pulled out his cell phone and activated the camera.

"I want you to see what others see." He snapped the photo and reviewed the image, his stoic expression made her stomach flutter anxiously. He flipped the phone around for her to see.

"Fuckin' unbelievably beautiful."

Her hands shook when she reached for the phone. She felt the breath knocked out of her.

Who was that woman in the photograph?

She could not recognize herself. Even with the streaks of paint on her hair and face, she looked like a sea nymph. Shades of green and blue kissed her skin and gave her an almost mythical effect. Her face looked radiant, youthful and…*happy?* Her eyes moved downward and she took in the artwork gracing her body. She sucked in her breath at the sight of Caleb's talents.

He had painted a cherry blossom tree across her abs. The cherry blossoms were nestled on delicate branches, some petals trickled downward, and a vine wrapped around the tree in a winding, erotic manner. She didn't know how to feel, what to think. He amazed her, inspired her, and the familiar ache seized her heart. Gripping so tight she could not imagine ever wanting to forget her night with him.

"Make love to me Caleb. I—"

"Shhh." He placed a finger over her lips. "Don't speak. Let me give you what you need. What we both need." Caleb grabbed the phone and threw it on the pile of clothes.

He slid between her thighs, his body weighing on her, and kissed her hard. His lips moved down to the curve of her throat, lower until he brushed them across her aching nipples. The brown peaks grew to pebbled hardness and he captured them between his teeth. Her skin tingled and a hot tide of passion rushed through her as he feasted on her breast, running his tongue around the areola. Biting, sucking, squeezing.

She gripped his shoulders, caressed the cords of his back, massaging gently and he moaned against her skin. The sound vibrated through her to her pussy and she pressed herself against his rigid shaft. One hand slid down her taut stomach to the swell of her hips.

She opened up for him like a budding flower and his eyes locked with hers. He pushed the head of his cock to the edge of her opening and she quivered in anticipation.

"There's no running from me," his husky voice warned.

She looked at him through her lashes, taunting him with her smile. "Not this time. I'm not going anywhere."

He plunged deep into her and an explosion of pleasure washed through her body. She squeezed, gripping snugly around his rigid shaft, holding him in place.

"Oh. My. God." He growled, claiming her lips as he moved between her thighs. With every stroke her skin sizzled and she moaned aloud with an erotic delight. She arched her back, digging her nails into his skin and he snapped, pounding into her, gyrating against her, spreading bliss through every pore.

She lifted her hips to take in every delicious inch of him. Together they found the tempo that bound their bodies, taking her to a place that was as sacred as the one she had created. He scorched her body with a powerful desire that overwhelmed her, made her want to weep.

Machiko felt her breasts crush against the hardness of his chest. She gasped and panted with every stroke. His movements were sweet agony as he pounded deep into her, so tight, fit so damn well. She was so wet that he glided easily inside her.

"More. Harder. I need more." She screamed, clawing at his back and he hissed.

His hands grabbed her buttocks, raising her hips for a better angle. He pulled out, quickly thrusting into her, so deep inside she wanted to cry from pure ecstasy. He was so big, so snug, filling her up, making her feel like his body was designed to fit hers.

The pressure mounted, building tighter and tighter until she couldn't hold on any longer. The cravings took hold and Machiko bit his shoulder, her teeth sunk into him. Hard. Harder. He let out a loud curse and pulled back. His mouth claimed hers and with one hard thrust he sent her tumbling on a slippery path of rapture until she screamed out her release.

Her body shook, wracked by sensations she had never imagined, never experienced before. The turbulence of his passion swirled around her, enveloping her in a sheath of pleasure and pain. The kind of pain that he had managed to unlock and liberated her from her own personal prison.

She felt limp, lightheaded, her spirit unable to fully come back into her own form. She didn't have to see Caleb to know he had quenched her thirst for fulfillment. His lips grazed her forehead, her eyes and his lips rested on her temple.

"No more running Hoshi." Caleb's hold tightened around her. "I know your secret. I know everything."

Chapter Eleven

"What did you call me?" Machiko's eyes flashed and she shifted out of his grasp.

"Hoshi Machiko Barrett-Kingston." Caleb watched her eyes narrow suspiciously. He reached for her and she pulled away, getting up off the slippery floor.

"Don't ever call me that again," she warned.

"What are you so afraid of? The past is in the past, this is the present."

"Just because you figured out who I am doesn't give you the right to pretend to understand me." She grabbed a nearby paint rag on the workstation and wiped off her feet, one at a time. When she was finished she threw the soiled fabric on the table.

"Give me a chance to get to know you then."

Caleb was confused by her reaction especially after what they had just experienced. Their lovemaking wasn't just two people fucking, it was a connection. He thought it was pretty damn electric!

He sat up for a better look at her. No matter how irritated he was with Mac, he couldn't deny that she was naturally striking. Nothing artificial about her, including her firecracker personality and unyielding stubbornness. In his eyes, every velvety inch of her was flawless, even when she gave him that wounded expression.

His only regret was his carelessness. He hadn't expected things to turn out the way they did. Normally, he was more level headed, responsible. He always took precautions for safety reasons but he had totally lost all sensibilities when it came to her. *Where's your head, Holden?*

Mac was the first person to challenge him mentally and physically. She didn't hand over any bullshit or sugar coat things like the women he had been with and a part of him was selfish. He wanted to have all of her, regardless of rationale and consequences. He wholeheartedly believed things weren't going to be *just* casual between them. No, not after what they shared. He sure as hell wasn't going to let her sully what they had done either.

He moved up off the floor, reached for his boxers and yanked them on. He would straighten things up and was anxious to get her back into his arms again. Make love to her again. Caleb headed straight for her, determined to work things out, but she stepped back to distance herself from him.

"I can't believe I trusted you." Her anguished voice was like a knife to the gut. He stopped dead in his tracks.

"Don't turn this around, Mac. I've never betrayed you."

"Listen to what you're saying. You snuck around and dug up my past without having the balls to ask me yourself. That's how you broke our trust!"

"I fuckin' shaved my head for you. If that isn't trust, I don't know what is!"

She ignored his outburst and planted a hand on her hip. "Tell me, Caleb. How did you find out about me?"

"Don't look at me like that. I'm an art lover. I know all the nuances of the artists I like. I have a voracious appetite when it comes to learning and my curiosity extends to following techniques and discovering the inspiration behind an artist's work." He inched closer.

She blinked at his words and searched his face for more

answers. "Then how did you get my painting?"

He held her gaze as he spoke. "You see, after high school graduation, my father took me to London on a father and son excursion. He had an incredible art collection and from an infant he taught me to appreciate art, obsess over it. We attended my first auction at Christie's. He knew I had a passion for collecting as much as he did. On that particular day, a painting was up for sale. God, I remember that day. They had unveiled this piece that totally blew me away." He paused for a moment.

His eyes drank in the sensuality of her standing there with attitude, completely naked with his drawing on her body. Soft lights filtered through the room and spotlighted her as if she was an artwork on display. Beautiful. Organic.

He cleared his throat, continuing, "When the auctioneer mentioned the painting was created by a thirteen-year-old prodigy, there was no doubt in my mind I wasn't walking out of that place without giving it a good shot. There was something so powerful, so unique about the color choices and imagery that I couldn't let someone take it home that day. I knew I had to have it." His gaze held hers as he said with confidence, "At any cost."

Her face softened at his story. "You liked my painting." She spoke those words as if she was stunned by the revelation. Caleb nodded, happy to be able to share this story with Mac, the artist who had fascinated him long before they ever met.

He rubbed his head as he conjured up the memories, recalling every detail of that day. Those feelings of exhilaration would never fade because those were one of the few last good memories he had of his father.

"I was so enamored by this particular piece I sold my soul. I begged my father to get it for me and swore I'd pay him back by agreeing to work in his company after college. Because of my passionate plea, he finally gave in. It was a grueling battle between my father and another man but in the end we got it. That's all that mattered…" His voice trailed off and he glanced back at her as if he had been struck by lightning.

"Oh my God. That night." He took a few steps forward to stand in front of her.

"Caleb, please don't."

He reached out and seized her upper arms. She looked away and he pulled her to him. "No. That's why you looked like you had seen a ghost. Holy shit. You saw the painting that hung back there, didn't you?"

Her eyes widened and he could see a shimmer of moisture forming. She nodded and he watched her bite her lower lip to control the tears. Damnit! Even now she tried to be in control.

"I loaned my sister that piece for the evening. It was one of her favorites. There were so many times we used to wonder whatever happened to you. You vanished into thin air after that scandal."

"Stop it!" She broke free of him. Her hands curled into fists and she pummeled his chest. He took every blow without wincing and watched the tears roll down her cheeks.

"Why, Mac? Why didn't you tell me the truth? I would never judge you. I would never turn my back on you."

She tried to pull away but his grip was firm. She spat angrily, "You're lying. No one will ever understand how I feel. Everyone hated me because of my vicious lies…and I deserved all of it!" She broke down, sobbing now.

He dragged her into him and he held her tight. Kissing her temple as her body wracked with tears. Stroking her back, never letting go. She needed to finally grieve the lost girl.

"Baby, I'm here. There's no more pretending. No more running." He stroked her hair and his heart lurched, squeezing tightly as he consoled her.

Now he was the one inside looking out. He let out a quick sigh of relief. Finally, he would be able to comfort her without feeling helpless like that morning. The memory of her weeping on the floor had been emblazoned in his mind.

Then, there were the dreams. Dreams that had woken him up many a nights and now he was given a chance to do everything he had sworn he would. He would make damn sure he would help her through whatever it was that plagued her.

He would save her. The one thing he wasn't able to do for his own father.

⚜

The warmth of the sun mixed with the cool breeze blowing in from the ocean made the awkward lunch more bearable for Machiko.

"I'm so glad you were able to spend the day with me." Gemma's bright smile made Machiko shift nervously in her seat.

"Sometimes it can be confining at home." She picked up her iced tea and guzzled as much of it as she could.

Gemma's brows knitted together. "I see. So, I was thinking we could do a little shopping. Would that be alright?" Her expression was cheerful and Mac wasn't sure how to respond.

She shrugged. "Alright. Whatever you want to do."

The blonde's smile curved into a tight line. She pushed her salad aside and leaned in. "Okay, I'm gonna cut through the pleasantries. Let's get the hell out of this place and find us a dive to knock down some beers. Maybe it'll help you loosen up. If Caleb likes you, there's gotta be something special. How about it?"

Mac laughed then. This beautiful woman was practically cracking her knuckles and throwing her cards on the table. She wasn't as uptight and stuffy as Mac had imagined.

"Thought you'd never ask."

"You and me, baby. We'll down some booze and talk about shoes. Gosh, I just made a rhyme." Gemma's laughter was as infectious as her personality.

An hour later they were comfortably seated at the bar counter of an Irish pub in Santa Monica. This was a hidden nugget of a dive that was tucked away on Second Street between all the specialty and retail shops.

The décor was simplistic with its mahogany L-shaped counter, contemporary furniture, and dim bar lighting. Mirrored alcohol endorsements were hung throughout the tiny space and Celtic knot trims lined the walls. A row of beer taps with inscriptions on the bowling pin style handles stared back at them as they sat on bar stools awaiting their second round.

Gemma shifted in her seat, her elbow on the edge of the counter in a relaxed pose. "My brother tells me you're having an art show at Luc's gallery."

"I haven't confirmed yet. I'm out of practice and still trying to make up my mind."

"Are you kidding me?" Her eyes widened and she leaned in close, blushing. "I saw the painting you gave Caleb. Oh, you're very good."

Mac blinked, not knowing what to say. No one had seen her paintings since she was thirteen and she wasn't sure how to react. She bit the side of her mouth, debating on how much of herself she was willing to open up about.

"Thank you. I didn't realize he showed you."

Her smile broadened. "Well, he didn't really show me. I dropped by unannounced and he was there and so was the painting."

The beers came and Mac felt a sudden wave of thirst. She took a hefty drink and set the glass down. "Why did you ask me to hang out with you?"

"I thought it you might need the company. It's always difficult to make friends when you're the new kid in town."

She played with the perspiration on her glass. "Caleb didn't put you up to this?"

"He might have asked. Does it really matter?"

Mac shrugged. "I could take it as an insult that he doesn't think I can't make friends of my own. However, I will take that up with him. I'm glad you asked me regardless of the reason."

Gemma warmed up to her. "If it's any consolation, I fed my son a ton of caffeine before I left. Caleb's going to have a hell of a time getting him to settle down."

"I can grow to like you." Mac raised her drink up and Gemma clinked glasses with her.

"You should seriously consider doing the art show. I've never seen anything like it before; and if I had half your talents I'd be jumping on it. Why the hesitation?"

"I'm not sure I'm ready to show my stuff to the world. I don't think it would be a good idea."

"In what way? I would think you'd want to share your creation to people who would appreciate it. I'm not as serious a collector as Caleb is, but I would love to own something so engaging, so sensual. *So* passionate."

Mac laughed at Gemma's comment. "Really? You could see all that in my painting?"

"Of course! It's brilliant. In fact, I was thinking: I'm designing a hot new shoe line that are totally naughty and I'd love for you to do a few large scale images as a backdrop for the show. Please tell me you'll do it." Gemma beamed, as if she was proud of coming up with the idea.

"I'll think about it." She didn't want to make any promises when she was set to leave in a few short months.

Gemma squealed, "How wonderful! It's a start. I am certain that you'll give in because I've got relentless down to a science."

She grinned at the enthusiasm, flattered by Gemma's interest and proposition. She couldn't believe what polar opposites the siblings were when it came to her art. Mac wondered if the woman knew of her brother's own artistic abilities. The cherry blossoms he had painted on her body had astonished her. Most collectors she knew of weren't artists themselves and this fascinated her.

The thought of his fingers playing across her skin made her body tingle. Not even forty-eight hours had passed yet she still craved his touch, wanted to indulge in him until he was out of her system. Would she ever completely be free of him? She hadn't intended for Caleb to see her that way, vulnerable and defensive, but he had turned the moment into something she hadn't prepared for.

Machiko finished her beer and indicated to the bartender to get another round. The day was young and she figured if she got enough drinks in her companion she would get a lot of questions answered.

Mac said thoughtfully, "Why did Caleb stop painting?"

She watched the woman grip her glass and a sadness washed over her. "How did you know he paints? No one knows."

"It was a lucky guess." She felt guilty for not telling Gemma the truth, but deep down she didn't think it was her secret to tell.

"He stopped painting the day our father died." She paused and her ocean blue eyes zeroed in on a spot on the counter.

"I'm so sorry. I didn't know…"

Gemma nodded her head, letting out a deep breath. "Caleb had studied in Florence after high school graduation. He had promised to work an apprenticeship at the investment firm but Dad told him to follow his dreams and study abroad. He thought it was Caleb's calling. They had argued over the incident because Dad was under a lot of stress at the time and needed the help."

Gemma choked up, dabbed at her eyes with the bar napkin and continued. "A little over two years into Caleb's art program, Dad collapsed of a heart attack. We called Caleb and he rushed back, but it was too late. He always blamed himself after that. He dropped out of school, packed his bags and came back home to be the man of the house. Dad's partner took him on and showed him the ropes."

Knocking back her drink without as much as taking time to exhale, Gemma gained the courage to finish the story. "Caleb never touched a paintbrush after that day. Maybe it was too painful a memory for him. He did, however, inherit Dad's precious art collection and continued the tradition, the hobby Dad loved so much."

Mac wasn't sure what to do. She sat awkwardly, trying to find the right words but nothing would come. She didn't have a lot of experience in these situations but she knew grief, and she knew what it felt like to have known loss.

She managed to mumble, "I never realized. I'm sorry."

"No. It's okay. Gosh, it's been a long time but we never talk about it. *He* doesn't want to bring it up and he definitely shuts down when I ask him to paint again. In a sense, Caleb probably believes he was to blame for Dad's death."

"Why would he think that? Your father would have wanted him to follow his passion. It doesn't make sense."

"Caleb is a lot like Dad. He's stubborn and his sense of responsibility has always been a strength and a weakness. He wants to take care of everyone and often forgets he should take care of himself. I guess he believed that indulging in what he loved most, painting, he had created a burden for my father who had to work twice as hard to fill the gap. Which really wasn't the case."

"He was punishing himself." Machiko's heart ached. She had felt the same way and had buried her own love as if it would lessen the pain, would help her heal.

Gemma nodded in agreement. "Unfortunately, he was punishing himself for the wrong reasons. Dad had a rare heart condition that could not have been corrected even if it had been diagnosed. If Caleb had stayed, he would not been able to save him."

"If he knows the truth, then why did he give it up?"

"I think painting was a connection he found with Dad. They understood the beauty of art and it was the one thing they could share together. If he continued painting, it would be a constant reminder that he would never have the opportunity to share that father and son bond again. It's just too painful for him."

They sat in silence for a few minutes while Mac soaked in what she had just learned. Somehow Caleb had a lot more in common with her than she had realized. She had never stopped to see the whole canvas, only glimpsed sections of the painting. She had only focused on bits and pieces of Caleb's personality because she was afraid of finding out the truth, that they were a reflection of one another. That she liked him more than she dared to admit.

She brought a hand to her stomach and felt the heat rise up her chest. Why did he choose her to be his canvas? In that split second her heart burst into a million stars and she knew the answer.

His trust.

He had given her the most ultimate trust. He had given her

an invaluable piece of artwork that the world may never see, except for her eyes alone.

⚜

Drenched in sweat from head to foot from the morning run, the only thing Caleb could think about was hopping into the shower and staying there indefinitely. Oh, he could almost feel the cool water beating against his back, feel the screaming muscles relax and sedated.

He pulled off his shirt as he stepped into his bedroom and froze in the middle of the room. His eyes were immobilized by the ethereal silhouette, clad in a transparent kimono, staring out at the ocean view through his window. She twisted around as if she could feel his presence and her charcoal eyes softened at the sight of him.

She knocked the breath out of him.

"Hope you don't mind I let myself in. I took it as an invitation since your door was unlocked." Her smile was as intimate as a kiss.

"Mac, I thought you didn't want to see me for a while."

"I changed my mind."

"You can't keep doing this. I'm not a yo-yo for you to play with whenever you feel the need. It doesn't work that way."

She moistened her lips. "You're absolutely right."

Mac undid the wrap tie and slipped off the kimono. The silky fabric slid to the floor, gathering around at her feet like rose petals honoring a goddess. He couldn't move, his eyes raked hungrily over her body and it took all his willpower not to push her up against the wall.

Desire raced through his bloodstream but he wouldn't react, couldn't let her continue to leave his head in a jumbled mess. He closed his eyes for a brief second to tame the hard-on she had triggered. When he opened them again he wasn't prepared to find her standing a few inches from him.

"Thank you, Caleb."

He gave her a confused look. "For what?"

"For giving me your trust." Her velvet tone only added to the painful erection.

"I don't understand."

She shook her head, wrapping her arms around his neck, moving closer until she planted a soft kiss on his lips.

Mac ran her tongue across his jaw. "I'll just have to show you what I mean."

Chapter Twelve

Caleb wondered if he had walked into a dream. One in which Mac was the seductive siren luring him into a forbidden world of sensual enchantment. Should he take what she was offering or risk plunging headfirst into an emotional madness?

She smelled so damn good. The familiar scent of cherry blossoms circled around them like magical fairy dust. The warmth of her breath against his neck was a sweet persuasion that coaxed him into accepting this dream.

He couldn't resist the temptation any longer and gathered her in his arms, pulling her tight against him. Her soft curves molded to the contours of his body, her lips scraped across his skin, her hands teasing him with unspoken promises.

His head swooped down to capture her mouth. He feasted upon those succulent lips, lingering, savoring every moment. His hands explored the hollows of her back, skimmed across her ribcage to rest at the swell of her hips.

Caleb raised his mouth from hers, he gazed into her eyes. "As much as I love your games of seduction, I don't have the willpower right now. All I can think about is being inside you, making love to you."

He swept her, weightless, into his arms and carried her over to the bed, easing her down gently. He stepped back and shed the rest of his clothes before covering her petite frame with his large one. She reached out, stroking a finger sensuously up and down his arm.

"Oh no. You don't get to take the lead this round." She lifted her leg, wrapped it around his waist and flipped him on his back to straddle him.

He grinned at her quick reflexes, curious to see what she had in store for him.

"Close your eyes," she commanded.

"And if I don't?"

"Then you'll get none of this." She wiggled her hips, rubbing herself against him. *Evil vixen!*

"You can be persuasive." He said hoarsely, "Okay, eyes closed."

This was a new side of Mac that he hadn't envisioned and he liked the kinky side of her. He could feel her leaning in close, whispering against his lips, "Don't move or else…"

Mac climbed off of him and came back seconds later, resuming her position, her weight pressing down on his stomach.

"No peeking."

Without seeing, he wasn't sure what she was up to but he quickly discovered she was using the wrap tie of her kimono to blindfold him.

"I didn't realize you had it in you."

"No talking. No touching." She brushed a kiss against the curve of his neck. "That's better. Now, you're going to have to trust me. Can you do that?"

He nodded, hanging onto his sanity by a thread. Mac buried her face against his neck, teased the tender flesh of his ear, flicked her tongue along the edge of his earlobes.

"You're killing me, dar—" He didn't finish his statement when her lips muffled his words.

She plunged her tongue between his parted lips, exploring

him in a way that was beyond innocent. When she sucked on his tongue, he groaned into her mouth and his dick turned rock solid. He was so aroused it hurt and he surely thought the circulation had been cut off to his brain from the pure delirium.

He couldn't control himself. Game or no game, he needed her with a desperation that seized him. Caleb ripped off the blindfold and threw it aside. He grabbed her face between his palms and kissed her with a savage intensity.

Mac responded to him with the same unleashed fervor. She ran her hands across his shoulder blades, his neck, his face. Her mouth was hot on him, their tongues mating with every stroke. He pushed back the silky strands of her hair and massaged her skull as they kissed.

He became so lost in her, lost in kisses that were a divine kind of ecstasy. *Christ, she tasted too damn sweet!* She reminded him of honeysuckle and springtime, of his youth and running across sprinklers, cartwheels and ice cream.

Every moment spent with her was freeing, invigorating. She made him feel alive and his spirit didn't feel so heavy with the daily burdens. In her arms he could almost see a future so different than he had imagined.

She conjured up all these memories in his head. Good and bad. Memories he tried to repress of those long forgotten years. While other kids his age were experiencing their independence, on a mission of self-discovery, he was tackling adult responsibilities and mapping out a solid future for his sister.

Mac broke from his kiss, questioning him between heavy breaths, "Why me?"

"Why not you?"

Her tone grew serious. "I need to know."

"Because you are a breath of fresh air in my smog-filled life. Mac, you may not know it, but you inspire me far greater than anyone I've ever known."

No words have ever rung truer. She had turned his world upside down the moment he laid eyes on her. Her quirky and unpredictable behavior reminded him to breathe. He had spent so much of his life working, womanizing to fill the emptiness, yet what he was doing was avoiding his own truth. He had run himself into the ground in the same manner his father had and he didn't even know it.

"You know this is temporary? I want you to understand that I can't offer you anything more than a few months. The rest will be yours to live when I am gone." Her eyes changed from charcoal to onyx, so dark he couldn't read her thoughts.

"It doesn't have to be that way."

She stated with finality, "It has to be that way."

Mac slipped through his fingers and her lips blazed a trail down his body, stopping at his hipbone. She settled between his legs and looked up at him. The wicked gleam in her eyes told him he was in for a wild ride.

He held his breath with painful anticipation. She reached for him, her hands locking around his hard cock. With slow deliberation, she took him into her hot, wet mouth.

So. Fucking. Good.

Oh, he wanted to come on the spot but there was no way in hell he'd miss being inside of her again. Fucking her senseless to make up for her putting him through the ringer of sexual frustration all these long weeks.

All thoughts flew out of his head when her mouth and hands worked into a rhythm. She stroked and squeezed him with an expertise that surprised him. Where the hell did she learn how to do these things? Her tongue and mouth were pure magic, bringing him to the brink and back so many times he was ready to grab her by the hair and drag her up.

Her tongue glided up and down his shaft, teasing the head, sucking gently while her hands continued the steady strokes. He moved his hips to the same tempo as her mouth. She took in all of him as he fucked her mouth, needing to come like a jet that was backed up and ready to explode.

Mac withdrew her mouth and crawled up his body with feline skills. Blood pumped through him with breakneck speed at the thought of surrendering to her. Her pouty lips, swollen from his rough handling, curved into a seductive smile. He opened his mouth to praise her beauty, but the words died on his lips.

She positioned herself over him, planted her hands on his shoulders, and without warning she impaled herself on his excruciatingly erect shaft. He groaned as pleasure raged through him at finally being inside her. No words could describe the mind-blowing sensations.

She moved her hips until she found the right position, rocking back and forth. He cringed, biting back the urge to take over, but her movements clearly proved she was the one in control. He felt her squeeze around him and her languorous strokes were the most delicious kind of hell.

Her nails bit into his shoulders as she picked up momentum. Up and down. Up and down. She panted loudly and he watched in wonderment as her breasts heaved to the pace of their lovemaking.

"Come for me, baby," he urged.

His hands explored the curve of her back, the soft lines of her waist, her hips. He gripped her thighs and guided her as she moved. He could feel the tension building, knew every part of her coiled tight, could feel her impending release.

She cupped his face, moving her mouth over his. Her feverish kisses left his mouth burning with fire and he wanted more. Wanted every sweet ounce of her. She shivered in his arms, her moans escalating until she screamed out his name, her body jerked and a wave of warmth coated him.

He gasped for air, couldn't hold on any longer. The pressure was so strong it ripped through him, bringing on a powerful release that led him closer to the stars and the heavens. Even closer to Machiko.

She belonged to him now. He knew there was no turning back once he sold his soul for a chance at keeping her. It was just a matter of time before she would see it his way.

※

Machiko snuggled against Caleb as their legs intertwined. Their passionate lovemaking still lingered in her mind, contentment and peace flowing through her. She felt the familiar stirrings again as her body ached to have him inside her. He was a drug that brought all her sexuality to the surface and the high didn't subside even after he had satiated her. Over and over again.

She had never been with a man who knew how to play her body like a guitar, plucking each chord until he figured out the perfect note. Figured out what would make her scream and lose control. She loved that he was tender, strong, yet gentle all at the same time.

They had tried many different positions without inhibitions or embarrassment. She knew she would be sore for days but in the end, the strenuous workout was well worth the aches and pains. Well worth all the heartache she would carry with her when she left.

She would still have the memories.

Memories for her to lock up deep inside to pull up again on those lonely nights in Paris. She would not fall apart now, not when she came into this knowing it was fleeting. She had no right to feel this way. He did not belong to her and she should take each precious moment at a time.

What time was it now? She needed to call Luc to tell him that she was going to do the art show after all. She wanted to do it for Caleb. Most of all, she wanted to do it to prove she could face the world again.

The alarm clock read seven-thirty and she had to get going soon. Machiko looked over at his sleeping form and couldn't resist placing a quick kiss on his lips. Daylight filled the room with a film of gentle radiant glow, his body illuminated by the morning halo.

She ran her hand over the smooth surface of his head. He was still clean shaven and the look was growing on her. Secretly she was pleased he had decided not to grow back his hair just yet. At least she wanted to remember him this way for a little while longer.

There was something rugged and intriguing about a man with a shaved head. He was hot as hell and the look gave him a bit of an edge. None of the pretty boy looks. *My very own bad boy*. She smiled and the airy feeling reached her toes.

She wanted him to make love to her again but thought it was best to leave before he woke. Some things were better this way. Knowing him, he would persuade her to stay and she would never get all her work done. Machiko slipped out of the covers, careful not to wake him.

Collecting her kimono, she watched him sleep for a few seconds more while she dressed and tied the robe together. She couldn't believe they had spent most of their acquaintance arguing. Her eyes lingered on his face. At least the pent up frustrations had been released in their passionate coupling.

The thought of him pumping hard and fast into her activated a sudden surge of desire that made her sex pulsate. Yes, she had to get out of there before she gave in and spent the entire day in his arms. She leaned over and grazed her lips over the top of his head. Her heart promised to make it up to him later tonight.

❦

"Is this new, Caleb?" Jordan pointed to the painting hanging over his fireplace.

Mac's gift.

He looked up from the stack of papers. "Yes. Someone I know recently gave it to me."

"I'm surprised. It's a pretty extravagant gift." She walked up to the painting for a better look. "Anyone I know?"

"Maybe." He shrugged and pretended to refocus on his paperwork. "Jordie, anything else I need to sign before you go?"

She twisted around and walked over to stand in front of him. "Thanks for doing this on your weekend. You know how dad gets when a big portfolio is on the line."

"No problem. I'll be in the office on Monday to take care of the loose ends." He gathered the papers together and handed it to her.

She reached out to take the paperwork; her manicured fingers paused on his hand. "You know, Dad was telling me how much he'd like for you to work onsite more. He misses you. *I* miss you."

Caleb pulled his hand out of her hold and stood up. "Look, Jordie. You know I don't like punching the time clock and I definitely hate following the rules. If I can't stroll into the office every day in my board shorts, that environment isn't for me. Besides, I am just as productive working from home and popping in for those occasional board meetings."

She pursed her lips. "I see. Have you moved on, Caleb? Is that why you can't stand working where I do? Or do you think I would make you feel uncomfortable?"

"C'mon, Jordie. That's not it at all."

She crossed her arms defensively. "Ever since the night of Gemma's event, you're a totally different person. I don't even know you anymore. It's like the sight of me repulses you."

He took her hands in his. There was no longer the spark between them, not even the need to undress her or have her in his bed. Strange how Mac had ruined it for any woman who held an interest in him from here on out.

"You know you're as stunning as ever, Jordie. It's not that. I've just had some time to re-evaluate things. I guess you can say I'm reorganizing my life and my priorities."

"Basically you're re-evaluating us?" Her lips quivered.

"The *us* part has been over for some time, including the physical part of our relationship. I just think it's better this way. For both of us."

He saw the tears brimming in her eyes. "Damn you Caleb! You're telling me you're discarding five years of our relationship just like that? Ever since you got wrapped up, in God knows what, you haven't been yourself. Why? Tell me the truth. I deserve that at least."

"You're right. I do owe you the truth. I'm seeing someone and she's making an honest man out of me."

He had never thought this would be possible but Mac had made him see some things about himself he hadn't known. He had been able to reopen old wounds and allow himself to feel again, to think of his father without the hollow ache.

He squeezed her hand. "I'm sorry. I never intended to hurt you."

Jordie slapped him soundly across the face, breaking away. "You're not going to get the best of me Caleb. I gave you *everything* and would have given you more. Anything you desired."

He knew she was wounded, angry. He was glad he could get it off his chest and now she would be able to heal. He had hurt her time and time again even when he tried to make it work, but deep down he knew she wasn't the one for him. She never was.

Her eyes turned cold, impassive. She straightened up, throwing her shoulders back. "Just know that when she tears your heart out and leaves you as torn as I am, I will still want you back. I love you. I always will. I'm not giving up without a fight." Jordan turned on her heels and left.

Caleb heaved a sigh of relief, his heart still heavy from his honesty but this was the only way. If he didn't tell her now, there would not be a chance of him repairing their friendship later. They had known each other for a majority of their lives and he didn't want to lose that part of their relationship. Her father was his dad's business partner, now his.

He had inherited half of the business and Caleb would keep his father's legacy intact regardless of Jordan's feelings. Business was business and their relationship was personal. Why, then, did he feel a tinge of apprehension digging in the back of his mind?

Chapter Thirteen

"You're glowing, Mac. I haven't seen you in a few days and you've got a different aura around you." Frankie gave Machiko a warm hug. "I hope you don't mind I stopped by unannounced."

"Not at all! Have a seat anywhere." She waved her hand and was struck by the fact that her place was in shambles.

"Clean much?" Frankie's musical laughter made her join in.

"I'm sure Luc will ban me from ever house sitting again."

Frankie waved her comment off. "It'll all be okay. I'll call in my girl to come by later, maybe get some reinforcement, and we'll get this place in tip-top shape in no time."

"That's very nice of you. So, I was thinking." Machiko paused. She couldn't believe she was about to step out of her comfort zone.

"I was thinking you might want to see my paintings. They're nearly finished but I would love it if you would take a look."

"That would be lovely, dear! I was hoping." The woman's high pitched response raised her spirits further.

Twenty minutes later Machiko worried she had made a mistake. Frankie hadn't said a word, just inspected the paintings with the critical eye of an art professor. The older woman finally stepped beside her.

Machiko raised her eyes and her heart melted upon seeing the tears glistening in the older woman's eyes.

"They're absolutely beautiful." Frankie choked up, "I'm so proud."

Frankie gave Machiko a motherly hug that left a lump in her chest. The last time someone had stirred such emotion in her was when her own father had seen the creation that now belonged to Caleb. A thirteen-year-old didn't understand the significance of the praise, had only been blinded by the darkness that shut her off from any truth.

The doorbell rang and she was jolted back to the present.

"I'll be right back." Machiko was glad for the interruption. She opened the door and the postmaster handed her a certified envelope. *That's odd.* She signed off for it and closed the door. The envelope was addressed to Hoshi Kingston with no return address.

Her hands shook as she tore off the seal and pulled out the linen paper. The familiar watermark of her family crest made her stomach queasy, the blood pounding hard against her brain. She began reading the beautifully written cursive with a heavy heart.

My Dearest Hoshi,

It's been a long time. I know that you never expected hearing from us again, but I didn't have a choice. If not for the urgency of this letter I would not have contacted you, except on your terms. We need to speak and it's important you find it in your heart to see me again. I love you. We both love you very much. Never believe otherwise. We've all suffered enough. Now it's time to heal.

Your loving mother,
Sakura Barrett-Kingston

Machiko fisted the letter and it crumpled in her hand. *How did they find me?* She had made damn sure they wouldn't find her, yet they still managed to. The bone-chilling ache settled over her again, but this time the pain had dulled a fraction. Somehow.

Her soul split in half and she longed for those days when she hadn't disappointed her family, yet she also knew her alienation had been for the best. They didn't deserve a daughter who betrayed them.

She swallowed back the tears, quickly folded up the letter in the envelope and stuffed it in her pocket.

"Who was that?" Frankie's voice carried from the studio.

"Oh, the mailman went to the wrong address." She wiped at her eyes and took in a deep breath to level out before getting back to her guest.

She walked into the room and witnessed the woman's thoughtful expression, her hands steepled together against her chin. "This is going to be the most talked about exhibition in decades!" Frankie's cheerful tone made her feel worse.

"I hope I'm not making a big mistake."

Frankie gave her an incredulous look. "You kidding me, kiddo? I think this is exactly what the art world needs. Shake 'em up a bit. God, I'm salivating to see what the critics are going to say about these."

Machiko tensed up. Her hands fisted at her side as the familiar knot tightened in her stomach. She had forgotten about the critics, the media. *Christ! What had she been thinking?*

❦

Everything seemed out of focus as she stumbled to the kitchen. Machiko grabbed another bottle of wine and after several sloppy attempts she managed to uncork the top, staggering back over to the living room to resume her binge drinking.

She stubbed her toe on the impractical metal statue and let out a curse.

The doorbell rang while she was rubbing the injury to calm the painful throbbing. She ignored the intrusion, hoping the person would get a clue and leave. She had already made one mistake by opening the door earlier today, she wasn't about to see a repeat.

The doorbell continued to buzz and the noise became a sharp pain knocking against her skull.

She yelled in response, "Stop! Stop! Alright, I'm coming!" The bottle of wine splashed as she hobbled over to door.

"Hey there, Mac." Gemma greeted her with a wide grin, and then her nose crinkled up as if she'd been hit by a skunk. "Whoa. Smells like ass in here. Not that I'd know. Wow, you look like hell."

Machiko swung the door wider, hanging onto the doorframe.

"Having a pity party for one?" Jordan's haughty smile made her want to punch the shit out of the woman.

She blinked, her eyes going in and out of focus. Machiko managed to slur, "Wh…what's the problem?"

Gemma grabbed the bottle of wine that was clamped between her underarm.

"Hey!" Machiko protested as Gemma looped her arm through hers, dragging Machiko inside with Jordan in tow.

"Jeez, woman." Gemma took in the filthy surrounding and gasped, "What could have possibly happened for you to disregard personal hygiene? At least you could have invited me over to join in on the fun."

"Funny. That's very funny but I don't need you here. Go away." Machiko swatted the air, pretending that she was still in control when she couldn't fully process her conversation.

"Look. Have a seat. I'll air out the place and get something else in your system besides alcohol."

She grabbed the bottle back and smiled victoriously. "I'm pur…perfectly content. Just leave me alone. I'll be okaaay." That was a lie. Her head started to throb and her body appeared a little off balance. She slid to the floor in front of the fireplace, clutching the wine as if it was a precious artifact.

"Sorry, but I'm not going anywhere. Jordan, help me. Jordan!" Gemma turned her head and didn't find the woman. Machiko watched her go in search of Jordan.

She tried to get up but her legs didn't want to cooperate with her body. The thought of Jordan running loose in her house pissed her off. Her heart pumped hard, her adrenaline kicking in. She scrambled to her feet and dropped the wine bottle in the process when she realized Jordan had gone into *her* studio.

As soon as she walked into the room a flood of anger arrested her. She demanded, "What are you doing in here?"

Jordan turned white as a sheet; a flash of something unreadable flitted across her eyes. "You. It's you."

"Get the fuck out of my house! Now! Do you hear me?" Her voice boomed so loud it had snapped her into momentary sobriety.

The beautiful brunette stormed out of the house and she didn't know whether to be relieved or embarrassed about her heated reaction. One moment she was smiling and the next the room seemed suffocating, moving far off in the distance like an endless tunnel.

Spinning, spinning, spinning.

She was losing her footing and couldn't stand up straight. Her arms flailed around, her head pounded brutally, and darkness engulfed her as soon as her eyes fluttered close.

৩৫৪

Machiko woke up feeling like she had gone several rounds with Laila Ali and lost. The searing pain made it difficult for her to lift her head up, even harder to sit up in the sofa. Her lips were so parched she could barely open them. She strained to speak; instead, she reached for whatever glass was on the coffee table. She guzzled the contents down so fast she almost choked, liquid dribbling down her cheeks and chin.

"Glad to see you're among the living." Gemma walked over to the sofa and handed her a red concoction.

She said hoarsely, "Tomato juice?"

"No way. Nothing cures a hangover like a Bloody Mary. Sorry, no celery."

She switched glasses with Gemma and gulped most of the

drink down, wiping her mouth on her forearm when she finished.

"Caleb was right. You need a lesson on feminine etiquette."

She rolled her eyes and leaned back against the cushion. "What are you still doing here?"

Gemma shooed her to scoot over and took a seat beside her. "Well, let me see. You hit the floor so hard that I felt the migraine you'd have when you eventually woke up."

"Thanks. I...I'm afraid I can't seem to remember anything after the third bottle of wine." She rubbed her temples to ease the pain.

"Well, you did a stellar job of getting rid of Jordan."

"Jordan was here? Here, in this house?" She couldn't remember a damn thing and it worried her.

"Yes. You were a tad bit pissed about her seeing your paintings." She giggled, "I was even frightened by the demonic voice coming out of that petite frame."

Machiko groaned. She didn't like knowing that a virtual stranger was taking liberties by entering her private sector, uninvited. Some things she could live with but knowing that Jordan had violated her personal space angered her. The vein on her temple ticked and she let out a few long breaths to calm herself.

"Did she say anything?"

Gemma shook her head. "Nothing I could remember. If she did, I didn't hear it."

Feeling a little guilty about her drunken behavior, she knew she would have to apologize to Jordan in the future. If she ever saw the woman again.

"It'll blow over. I've known Jordan since I was a little kid and she's always been a bit snoopy. Look, I would've been upset too if someone went somewhere they weren't supposed to. It was disrespectful and I'm sorry." Gemma cast her eyes on the coffee table.

Machiko decided to let things go. After all, she was the first friend who witnessed her idiotic behavior and stuck around. She twisted her neck to look at Gemma. "Thank you. Thanks for being a friend."

She could have sworn Gemma blushed and her radiant smile was enough for her. Machiko couldn't help grinning back, pleased that they understood each other.

Machiko settled her head back to face the room and the pungent smell of cleaning products filled her nostrils. Her eyes darted around the room. She noticed the place was sparkly clean and bolted upright, taking in the complete surroundings. "You cleaned my house while I slept?"

Gemma shrugged. "It's a mommy thing. I had years of practice so it came in handy tonight. Unfortunately, you're on your own with the dry paint stains in your studio."

She had to laugh at that comment. There was no chance of her ever telling Gemma the truth. Some things were just too personal.

A warm glow filled Machiko's spirit. Life had changed so drastically since moving here and she certainly experienced more in a few weeks than she had in a lifetime. She was amazed how simple it was to allow herself to meet new people. Something she had never believed possible.

In the years after she left the facility, she had become an introverted individual who was always on edge. Frankie and Gemma had accepted her idiosyncrasies and liked her anyway.

She grew suddenly serious. "I've never had a friend before…" her words faded. Her face grew hot from embarrassment.

Gemma reached for Machiko's Bloody Mary and took a drink. "We all need friends. You never know when you might need one to hold your hair back when you throw up after a long night of alcohol induced debauchery. Now that's a good friend."

She was grateful for Gemma not turning the situation into an awkward moment. Machiko scrunched her face and replied, "Sounds great. Sign me up."

Gemma burst out laughing. The action was so contagious she found herself joining in and their laughter carried through the house. She really enjoyed another woman's companionship and

Caleb's thoughtful reasons that brought this woman into her life.

Machiko grinned from ear-to-ear. She realized what they were sharing had made up for all those lost moments she had been deprived of as a child. Today was a new chapter and she hoped there would be many more happy ones to come.

✤

"Keep your eyes closed and watch your step." Caleb warned as he helped her out of the car and led her down a winding path.

"If this is some sick way of getting back at me..." she grumbled, but her curiosity was eating away at her insides. She was never good at surprises of any kind.

"Never. What kind of guy do you take me for? I'm shocked," he feigned a wounded voice.

She opened her mouth and he yanked on the bow of her blindfold, the silky fabric sliding off her eyes. Machiko gasped as she watched the twinkling lights below, could see the steady flow of traffic buzzing down the freeway like streams of Christmas lights flipping off and on.

She sucked in her breath, stunned by the beauty of the city. This secluded little section was a perfect romantic spot. Private enough to do whatever they wanted without being detected. She wondered how he came to find this place.

Caleb's arms encircled her waist, and she leaned back against him, his chin rested on the top of her head. They stood silently, sharing the peacefulness and enjoying the scenic view. She felt like she was on top of the world and being with him was the cherry on top.

He kissed the side of her head. "What do you think?"

Machiko brought his hand up to her lips and pressed a kiss into his palm. She grinned and twisted in his arms, tilting her head back for a good look at him. She thought she could see specks of light reflecting in his toffee eyes.

"You're something else, Holden. I hadn't pegged you as the

romantic type."

He snorted then kissed the tip of her nose. "That's because I never know what to expect—Doctor Jekyll or Miss Hyde."

"Very funny. Are you trying to seduce me?"

"Is it working?" He nuzzled her neck, his lips brushing her skin and she melted into his embrace.

"Maybe. Just. A. Little." She sighed, loving his attention.

Her skin prickled pleasurably when he swirled his tongue along the tender spot behind her ear, moving upward, across her jaw line until his mouth covered hers.

His kiss was tender, his tongue probing, his fingers drawing little circles up and down her back. She could feel her toes curl from the erotic ministrations, making her moist with need. The thought of making love in this intimate location, out in the open, sounded daring, quite enticing.

She planted airy kisses on his neck, and inhaled against his soft skin, suddenly drugged by his clean and masculine scent.

"You smell good enough to devour." She purred.

"Well, then I should feed you. Maybe you'll have the energy to work off the dessert." He turned her body and moved along with her.

Her heart thundered at his unexpected thoughtfulness. He blew away any of the dates she had ever considered romantic. Machiko's eyes took in the exquisite setting comprised of a comfortable blanket covering a small patch of earth.

White candles sat on a three-tiered, metal holder in the center of the blanket which gave the area some soft illumination. Fine chinaware was laid out with several food carriers placed between the settings. A bottle of champagne sat nearby in a stainless steel chiller ready to be served and next to the object was a portable CD player.

Caleb laced his fingers through hers and she followed him to the romantic picnic. They took a seat on the plush blanket and she tried really hard to refrain from throwing herself at him before they even made it to the first course.

"Let's loosen you up." He teased before preparing their drinks.

He skillfully uncorked the bottle, filling the champagne flutes before handing her a bubbly glass. He lifted his hand in a toast. "What should we drink to?"

Was this their first real date? Feeling a bit shy, she looked at him through her lashes and caught a twinkle of moonlight in his eyes. Caleb had outdone himself this time but she wasn't going to complain. The entire planning and execution had proven to her what a remarkable man he was, so very thoughtful and sexy as hell.

He snapped his fingers. "Got it. To us." He grinned, showing perfectly straight teeth.

"To the moment." She clinked glasses with him.

He took a sip then leaned in to kiss her. His mouth was wet, cool, and refreshing as she tasted the sweetness on his tongue. As he kissed her he unbuttoned her blouse and she didn't realize what he had done until she felt the cool night breeze against her skin.

"You're good." She ran her tongue along his lower lips.

"Not half as good as you're going to taste."

He held the flute up and poured a few drops down her chest. She squealed as the cold liquid made a slow descent between the hollows of her breasts, trickling onward. He bent his head, his tongue following the path of the champagne and she squirmed.

He took her flute and put their glasses aside. Caleb gave her a devilish smile before he slipped between her thighs, bending her backwards until her head was cushioned on the thick fabric. He pushed her blouse open before continuing where he left off. His hand cupped her breast, squeezing and molding it beneath the lacy fabric.

A moan escaped her lips and he nipped at a pebbled peak, plucking at it with his teeth through the thin fabric. She arched her back, wanting more. His gaze traveled over her body as he continued massaging her breast. A spark of lust flashed across his eyes and he shoved her bra up, his mouth covering a swelled breast.

He indulged himself, licking, biting, teasing one breast then the other. He moved up her body and captured her lips, his kisses passion-filled. His tongue forceful as he explored her mouth and then his hand glided up to rest on the base of her throat. The simple act made her pussy swell, throbbing and wet for him.

She couldn't explain how fucking hot she felt with him taking control. She trusted him and knew he would never hurt her, but the gentle pressure of his hand on her throat heightened her desire.

Machiko kissed him with the same hunger, couldn't get enough of him. Her nails clawed at his chest and back as if she meant to fight him. He groaned against her mouth and she knew this sexual game worked him up as much as he had her.

"I want you to fuck me." She wasn't shy in her request.

"God, you're so fuckin' hot when you talk to me like that." He crushed his mouth against hers, biting her lower lip, his tongue showing her just how he wanted to make love to her.

They were both panting and breathing heavily when he rolled off of her then he undressed her. Their clothes flew in a heap on the ground.

"I'm not going to be gentle," he threatened.

She answered breathlessly, "I wouldn't want it any other way."

He gave her a wicked grin and ran a hand down her taut stomach to the swell of her hips, sliding in between her thighs. He cupped her cheek and pressed his lips to hers, kissing her softly, gently this time.

She writhed beneath him, wiggling her hips and he let out a tormented groan before he nudged her thighs wider and plunged deep into her. She gasped, raising her hips, wanting as much of him as she could take. He moved inside of her slowly at first then the momentum kicked up.

His cock was so big and hard, filling her up. Pounding into her, twisting his hips as he pulled out, ramming back inside. She wanted to explode every time he repeated the motion. He made her feel things that were indescribable. Her body felt like it was transported on a soft and wispy cloud, floating higher and higher.

With every stroke she became more aroused, climbing closer and closer to a fiery release that eagerly awaited her. She moved with him, their bodies bound together, dancing to the music of the night that only they could hear.

They made love under the stars and moon as the city below hummed softly, creating their song, wrapping them in a magical halo of unspoken promises.

Tonight she was completely his. Tomorrow she would be ready to face the demons she had kept at bay for too long.

Chapter Fourteen

Machiko stood outside waiting. *Where was he?* She paced the length of the house and back. She grew tired of counting the stones in the cobbled path, isolating the colors, outlining the shapes with her eyes. After a few minutes she gave up and took a seat on the wooden steps. Waiting.

A few seconds ticked by and she wrapped her arms around her legs, drumming her fingers against her skin. She jerked when her cell phone vibrated.

Damn cell phones! She hadn't gotten used to the thing since Caleb had given it to her the night of the picnic. Why would someone want to be tied down to what was basically a modern tracking device?

Fumbling to decipher the devil's gadget she managed to answer the call, and let out a frustrated breath. "Hello."

"I still can't believe you caved in. Congratulations on catching up to speed with the technology age!" Luc's charming French accent was always comforting.

"*Bonjour, Luc!* Where are you? When are you getting here?"

"I'm just a few minutes away. If you look up, you might be able to catch a glimpse of me in the unattractive rental."

She laughed knowing full well that Luc had far better taste than any straight man should.

"I think I see the station wagon coming around the bend. I've only been gone a few months and you've turned into a family man. Small wonders!"

"Where is the sweet and innocent Machiko I know?" He mocked, "I gather Caleb has taught you the fine art of verbal sparring."

"You didn't think I had it in me? So little faith."

"*Ma petite fleur*, I'll test the theory in person. *À bientôt*."

She ended the call and tucked the phone back in her pocket. Leaning back on her elbows against the upper steps, she glanced around. There seemed to be no signs of life as she looked down the perfect row of houses neighboring this one. No laughter, no children, nothing remotely inspiring.

Machiko honestly believed technology was the reason why children opted to stay indoors and obsess over video games, rather than playing outside. Those were the things she missed out on as a child but under totally different circumstances. Her lips curved into a frown. She would have loved to have experienced a real childhood.

These days, she enjoyed her freedom and disconnecting herself from life's distractions. She never cared for watches or keeping track of time and found herself more productive that way. Life was too short. In allowing time to dictate her day it created limitations and complications.

Saisissez le jour. Seize the Day. She had learned to follow this philosophy during her ten years of independence: picking up and going wherever her heart desired, working in whatever menial job she could pick up to stay under the radar. She never needed the money, but after five years of repression, she needed to face society. Needed to interact with real people after living in a controlled bubble.

In truth, Machiko was fortunate that she had never known poverty or faced financial hardships. Her paintings had brought her an unimaginable amount of wealth. Her trustee had maintained her finances and allocated her funds, advised her on investments and monitored her portfolios until she was twenty-five years of age. When she had full access to her funds, she had elected to continue to retain the trustee's expertise.

She was twenty-eight, no longer a child, but barely a woman who had lived through the bad experiences that shaped her into the person she was now. Time had taught her to differentiate the good apples from the bad. She had known them all in her journey. The con artists, the manipulators, the greedy and obsessed. That was the reason why she masqueraded as someone else, someone normal as a way for her to escape the attention. Those days were over now.

Her only wish was to be left alone, yet she knew deep down her life would never be "normal".

Machiko spotted her friend and watched as the sleek black Roadster pulled in front of the house. Machiko jumped up and ran toward her friend. She gave him a big hug as he swung her around in a circle as if she were a child.

He was a sight for sore eyes. Luc Delacroix was a handsome man who was often mistaken for a younger Jean Reno. His warm and humorous personality had pulled her out of her shell during her awkward beginnings. In time she had come to view his family as her own, and Luc took on the role of friend, mentor and surrogate father.

Luc kissed Machiko soundly on both cheeks. "It is great to see you looking so well."

"I'm sad your wife and children couldn't make it."

"There will be plenty of opportunities, *non?*"

She frowned. "I do miss them, but you're right. I'll call later and try to persuade them to visit."

"You see, you have it all figured out. *Alors*, I'll get my suitcases later. For now, I would like to see what chaos you have been working on for me." He swung an arm around her shoulders and they headed into the house.

❧

Caleb watched the interaction between Luc and Mac at the

dinner table and felt a twinge of jealousy. *Don't be ridiculous, Holden!* He continued to watch but still didn't like the thought of someone else receiving her attention. His brows creased together. He wished she would give him a look with the same adoration.

Damn it, he had no right to be wound up about it. He and Luc had been friends for years and he knew the man was happily married. So why, then, was he so pissed off? Whatever it was he had the urge to drink. A lot.

When Mac said something endearing, Luc patted her cheek and they continued discussing the preparations for the art show. Caleb clenched his fists, could feel a tick pulsing at his temple.

What the hell is the matter with you? You're acting like an ass. He picked up the wine glass and drained the liquid, setting it back down without even a blink.

He clucked his tongue as he watched. Mac had gone to great lengths to prepare an elaborate dinner that was complete with candles and a centerpiece of orchids. A little too intimate for his taste.

Frankie cleared her throat and his eyes darted across the table to meet the older woman's gaze. She leaned forward, motioning to him with her eyes for some privacy. Appreciating the diversion, he followed her lead and focused his attentions on her.

Frankie whispered, "She's quite beautiful, isn't she?" Her eyes fixed on his face as she raised her glass, peering at him over the rim as she sipped on the wine.

He returned his gaze to Mac, a hint of a smile forming. "I have to agree with you there."

His heart skipped every time he saw her. He wanted to kiss her so bad his body twitched just thinking about it. The other night had been an awakening for him and since then he couldn't get her out of his head.

Caleb grabbed the wine bottle and topped her glass off before refilling his.

Frankie clasped her hand in front of her. "Why don't you tell her then?"

"Tell her what?"

"Tell her you love her. Tell her you want her to stay." Her steady gaze held his.

How could he respond to that suggestion? He wasn't even sure what he was feeling was "love". Yes, he wanted her. He enjoyed making love to her. He found her challenging, yet thrilling. She was all those things that made him want to be with her, but how could he be certain the emotions were love?

Luc leaned back in his seat and looked over at them. "Frankie, how are your projects coming along?"

"Glad you should ask." Frankie winked and focused her attentions on Luc.

They had a lengthy conversation on her current hobby of antique restoration and Caleb was relieved he didn't have to answer her. He watched Mac pick up the dirty plates and he found it the perfect opportunity to spend a moment with her. He grabbed a few dishes and followed her into the kitchen.

Mac placed her stack in the sink and he came up behind her, one hand on her waist, the other disposing of his dishes in the sink.

"Hey, you. Thanks for the assist." She twisted in his arms, tilting her head for a better look.

He stood speechless.

Her cheeks were rosy from the affects of the alcohol, her skin flawless without any trace of makeup, her lashes so thick and dark it enhanced her midnight eyes. She captivated him more every time he saw her beautiful face.

She was a picture of youthful innocence in her rock band t-shirt and white capris. So much that he couldn't resist wanting to do wicked and sinful things to her. Caleb felt like a man burning with lust. He was burning in the eternal pits, and Machiko was his only salvation. He would gladly suffer the tortures for just one kiss.

Caleb bent his head to claim her lips with a ferocity he hadn't expected. Kissing her as if his life depended on it, as if he could wipe away memories of any man who had kissed her before him. His tongue probed and teased, leaving nothing unexplored.

She broke away from their kiss. "What's gotten into you tonight?"

"I can't help myself. You're so beautiful. Let's get out of here." He cupped her cheeks, stroking her face with his thumbs.

The suggestion sank in and she blushed. "You know we can't. We've got guests. Besides, it would be rude."

"Afraid of getting caught?" He didn't wait for her answer. He grabbed her waist and lifted her onto the edge of the sink. She let out a squeal, wrapping her legs around him.

"You're insane!" She gripped his shoulders to steady herself.

"Kiss me," he commanded in a husky voice.

She slid her arms around his neck and ran her tongue slowly across his bottom lip.

"Is this what you want?"

"You know what I want." His cock pressed tight against his jeans and he couldn't concentrate on the game.

Her lips brushed against his as she spoke, "Tell me what you want."

Caleb kissed her hard, cruelly ravishing her mouth, and she moaned in response. His hands explored her hips, moving upward to the small of her back. She arched forward and he felt her heat warming his torso. His kisses never eased knowing her excitement and how wonderful she would taste once he stripped her naked.

Frankie let out a surprised gasp, "Oh dear."

They jerked apart. Caleb's brain was still cloudy from the thrill of the kisses.

"We're caught." He grinned at Machiko and could feel the warmth of her body flush from embarrassment.

"Well I see you took our conversation to heart. Carry on," Frankie laughed, hastily retreating from the kitchen.

He smacked her on the butt. "Let's get back. I can't believe you tried to seduce me," he teased as he helped her down.

"You're so going to beg for it later." She faked a kiss and ran off.

Taking a few seconds to adjust himself, Caleb didn't think he could sit through another thirty minutes of pleasant conversation. Either he had to relieve himself of the frustration or he was going to resort to cavemen tactics and drag Machiko out of the house by her hair. He chuckled knowing damn well she would fight him tooth and nail if he even looked at her the wrong way. *That's my girl.*

Caleb walked in as Mac, Luc and Frankie were absorbed in their conversation about the guest list and the publicist.

Luc smiled up at him. "Let's step out on the deck for a bit."

He nodded. "Too much estrogen in the room without me?"

The women groaned in unison.

"I had a sudden urge for some air, though I regret leaving the company of such beautiful women." Luc stood up and tipped his head. "Excuse me for a moment."

Mac gave him a disappointed look. "I thought you quit smoking."

Luc winked. "I didn't say I was going for a smoke. I wouldn't dare try because I know you would never stop nagging me until I returned to Paris."

Her eyes twinkled mischievously. "Right. Did I mention I'll be doing a smell check as you walk back in?"

"Let's get out of here before she decides to rope and tag us, too." Caleb quickly led him out of the house. He could hear the women's laughter as they stepped onto the deck.

Luc took a seat on the swing and Caleb joined him. The man looked around guiltily and withdrew a pack of chewing gum from inside his jacket pocket.

"Care for one?"

Caleb shook his head. "You really did quit."

Luc frowned, rolling his eyes. "You may have discovered how persistent Machiko can be. I have had, er, experiences in which she has traumatized me by helping me quit smoking."

He shivered at the thought, knowing firsthand what her temper and stubbornness was like. Caleb settled back in the swing.

Luc popped the two pieces of gum in his mouth and tucked it back into his jacket pocket. "You have questions about

Machiko, *non?*"

"You're damn right I do. I'm just wondering why you've never spoken about her in all the years I've known you."

Crossing his legs, Luc let out a momentary breath. "When she first came into my home I wanted to refuse her services. She was not the usual au pair and had no real qualifications. But one look at her face, the emaciated frame, I couldn't turn her away." He paused as if remembering that day. "How could I allow someone so broken to leave my home without giving her a chance? She was barely nineteen and all alone. She had no family and no friends. My wife and children loved her instantly. They must have felt the same way I did. After enough time, I could see her come out of her shell."

"You still haven't answered my question, Luc."

"I respected her wishes. She asked me to give her privacy and wanted anonymity. I could tell she had trust issues and I have always honored her request. Until..."

Caleb swung an arm over the top of the swing. "Until?"

"It was three years ago, I believe. Machiko had taken the children out to the park and I had gone into my daughter's room to see if she had run off with my favorite tie. I rummaged through her closet and discovered Machiko's paintings." He straightened up, his hands gesturing as he spoke. "Magnificent artwork was hidden there like she was a child stowing away a secret. God, Caleb. They were so incredible, so vulnerable, so raw and full of pain. I know talent and Machiko was born with that gift. How could she deny the world such beauty? It angered me that she had hidden this as if she was ashamed of her own abilities."

"I can imagine it didn't settle well with you. You're right; Mac does have a problem with trust." He rubbed his jaw.

Caleb remembered how difficult it must have been for her to come to him. In knowing that about her, he was pleased and felt privileged she had chosen him to give her trust.

"Not long ago I approached her. I could not stay silent any longer and asked her about the paintings. She was so upset she wanted to leave us. The children begged her to stay and they resented me for hurting her."

"You were in a tough spot, Luc."

"I gave her time to calm down and then she acted as if we had never spoken about her. About her past." Luc's face appeared thoughtful, his eyes drifted off into the distance.

His eyes met Caleb's and he could see the seriousness of his expression. "There is something I need to tell. Something I'm not proud of."

"What could be so bad?"

"I hired someone to learn everything about Machiko's identity. Her family is alive and I even went so far as to meet them. I know why she is the person she is."

Caleb let out an exasperated breath. "That makes two of us."

His friend's brow raised in interest. "What do you know, Caleb?"

"I hired someone, too. You know how obsessed I am with technique. Mac had given me a painting. It drove me nuts because I had seen some similarities to another artist. I just couldn't put a finger on it. You don't know how foolish I felt when the answer was sitting under my roof. I owned her original artwork from that day in London."

Luc nodded, a wide grin on his face. "The day with your father and the auction. *Oui*, I believe my father gave yours a good fight. You know how upsetting it was for me to lose such a prize."

"Will you tell her about her parents?" Caleb crossed his arms.

"*Oui*. When the time is right. I wholeheartedly believe once she gets over the pain she will realize she needs them. She deserves her family as she has given mine so much. I don't realize she knows her emotions all comes down to one thing—"

Mac presence interrupted Luc's dialogue when she stuck her head out the door. She eyed them curiously. "Dessert. You two interested?"

The dessert Caleb wanted could not be shared with others. His mouth watered at the thought of her sprawled naked on his bed, trembling for his touch. Seeing her face made his stomach constrict, his dick rose to attention with breakneck speed. He shifted uncomfortably.

He decided he would risk her wrath, steal her away to show her how much she aroused him, how proud that she was going to do the art show.

Mac the girl was growing into Mac the woman, blooming right before his eyes.

Chapter Fifteen

Machiko's stomach churned as she took a quick glance at her reflection in the mirror. She had spent the past three month putting finishing touches to her paintings in preparation for the art show. This morning Gemma had dragged her out of the house at the crack of dawn, had taken her to a spa, then to see her makeup artist and hairstylist. Her protests had fallen on deaf ears. Now, she stood completely transformed, waiting nervously for the event to commence.

She turned away from the mirror and smoothed her emerald, floor-length gown. The style was unique with the purposefully wrinkled fabric across the chest and tapered to an empire waist. The crinkled straps hung loosely below her shoulders, the material light and translucent as it flowed down to form a small train.

Her messy curls were styled in a Grecian updo with pearled ribbons in shades of green woven throughout her hair. Her makeup was dark to highlight her features and she was confident no one would ever recognize her as the little girl who had once opened up her own show. Machiko never had the need to dress up but she was grateful for the intervention.

She hadn't seen Gemma until she crossed through the room and clasped her hand. "Ready, Mac?"

Her body was paralyzed with fear, her speech stolen for a brief second. Machiko finally nodded and mustered a faint smile.

"You're shaking. Take a deep breath. That's it." Gemma squeezed her hand for good measure. "I know you're not a fan of crowds but you look amazing. Your paintings are out of this world and everything will be over in no time at all."

Gemma didn't let go of her hand. She led Machiko out of the room, guiding her down the hall. They stood at the entrance and Gemma let go of her hand to nudge her through the gallery doors that led into the substantial space.

As soon as she entered, light bulbs flashed around her and the media threw a barrage of questions her way. Luc and his publicity team had managed to generate quite a media buzz and the guest list had included major celebrities and pillars of the community.

All the attention and scrutiny made her head swim with confusion and trepidation and her throat constricted. She felt a wave of queasiness and a bit suffocated by the size of the crowd.

She wanted to run and hide. Her eyes darted around for an escape route. Growing terrified she shifted in place, trying to back up when she was halted by a solid form. She craned her neck and relief flooded her instantly.

Caleb placed his hand on the small of her back. "Thank you for coming. Since this is Machiko's first show, I'm sure she will be happy to answer questions later once she's greeted her guests."

The media moaned and complained but backed down. Caleb escorted her past the throngs of people to a more secluded section of the room.

He rubbed her arms and peered into her eyes. "You okay?"

She took a deep breath and nodded. "I'm okay now that you're here."

Caleb kissed her forehead. "Good. Are you up to greeting everyone?"

"Yes. You aren't going to leave me?" Her voice rose in alarm. She didn't think she could make it through the night without his strength.

He placed a hand on her waist. "Of course not. I'll be with you every step of the way. I won't leave your side, I promise."

She believed him, her body relaxing against him. Caleb was the reason she wanted to confront this crowd and proved to herself she could overcome her anxieties.

Machiko cast her eyes upward, focusing on his face. Her heart was heavy with an emotion so powerful she wanted to weep. She caressed his cheek and pulled his face toward her for a tender kiss. She loved the feel of his lips. Loved the way their lovemaking seemed so natural and pure.

"Okay, let's get this over with." His eyes darkened with a forbidden lust and his tone seductive. "For my own selfish reasons."

The night became a blur of names and faces. She managed to answer the interview questions without any major hang ups. Her nerves faded and she became more confident about pulling this event off. Her feet ached and while Caleb was engaged in conversation with some guests she took the opportunity to view her paintings.

She had participated in many shows in her youth but seeing her art spotlighted on the walls seemed surreal, almost as if this was the first time she showed her work. Her eyes lingered over the miniature silver plaque which displayed the title of the painting and her name. *Machiko Barrett.*

The cloud lifted and a new joy replaced the heaviness in her heart. She no longer sensed the little girl lurking in her shadow, hiding from the world that had once praised her and then was quick to condemn her. She had reinvented herself.

Luc's voice filled the room as he used a nearby pastry knife to clink on his glass. She turned to face her friend, along with the rest of the guests. He was dressed in a fitted dark Armani suit and his entire demeanor changed. His easy going nature was replaced by a sophisticated and professional visage.

"Ladies and gentleman, thank you for coming tonight. This

show means a great deal to me and I hope it will be one that you remember for years to come. This artist has provided an exceptional look at the power of femininity. She captures a youthful eroticism, filled with emotional turmoil that leaves you longing to discover her artist's message." He paused and raised his glass. "I propose a toast to the amazing Machiko Barrett on a successful showing."

The crowd followed suit and raised their glasses, praised her talents, and enjoyed the sparkling liquid.

Luc lifted a hand up to quiet the guests. "Originally I was going to keep this a secret, but I feel the news is too incredible not to announce." He took a deep breath, his face beaming with pride. "It's my pleasure to reveal that this show has sold out!"

The crowd broke into gasps and hushed whispers. Machiko stood completely stunned. Who could have purchased her work? How was this possible? *Caleb*. She whirled around to meet his gaze and his expression was grim.

"I don't suppose…" She placed her hand on his arm.

"No. I didn't have the opportunity," he answered dryly.

She could see the anger brewing in his eyes.

Luc cleared his throat. "May I present Ms. Jordan Fenley, who represents the anonymous client."

Her cheerful mood veered sharply to sour. Something wasn't right and all the tragic memories came pouring down around her.

Jordan wore a classic black gown; her hair swept up into a sleek French twist, her stance reminded her of a beauty pageant contestant. "Thank you for the opportunity to speak on my client's behalf. This artist is a person whose value is immeasurable. We could not be happier to discover her latest showing. We are even more excited to discover her true identity. Miss Barrett may have drastically changed her artistic style but there is no denying her paintings reveal the same technical expertise of the prodigy the world has known." Jordan looked over at Machiko with a sardonic expression that sent her temper soaring.

Jordan continued her statement, eyeing Machiko with cold

triumph. "To own any piece of Hoshi Kingston is a privilege and an honor. We hope it will garner great returns with what we have in mind for it."

Caleb had a strong hold on her waist but she forced herself away, stepping toward Jordan. She was so furious she was seeing red. "You will never have any piece of me," she sneered.

"I'm sorry, Miss Barrett, but we now own all of you." Jordan's mouth curved into a cruel smile.

"Not if I can help it." Machiko's eyes locked on a pastry knife on a nearby table. She marched over and grabbed the object.

Jordan shrieked, ducking behind Luc when she realized Machiko was headed toward her. She couldn't control the anger that flooded all of her rational thinking. She had no intentions of aiming for Jordan; her only mission was to strike where it hurt most. She whizzed past the woman, plunging the knife into a nearby painting.

Her response had shocked the guests and soon flashbulbs went off like the Fourth of July around her. The crowd scattered, some stepping back as Machiko made her way to assault as many paintings as she could reach. She slashed her paintings with a vengeance.

No way in hell would she allow Jordan to leave with any of her work! Her paintings would never belong to a company that was only concerned with image or investment. Machiko would rather see her sweat and tears in the hands of an art lover who valued her work, was passionate about her creations.

Someone like Caleb.

She could not stand by while a corporate investor destroyed her vision and took away the reason she painted. She did not go into seclusion to be faced with this result.

Laughter ripped through her as her veins throbbed with a new understanding. In her mind's eye she could see the madness whirling around in her head, thoughts of a child who had no control of her actions. Tonight, she was in control. She knew her reputation was at stake but she reacted on principle alone. She was in charge and nothing, or no one, could ever take that feeling away from her.

Machiko did not see Luc and Caleb's intervention. Did not realize Caleb took the knife away, did not realize she had slipped to the floor as he consoled her. As if a dam had burst, she cried for all her past mistakes.

Tears of hate, anguish, and sorrow washed away as she embraced her past. She had stopped running, would no longer run away from her fears. She was free at last. She was finally purging the broken girl from her soul.

You know what you must do, Machiko.

She buried her face against Caleb's chest and wept for all the lost years as he held her tight, rocking her gently, stroking her hair. Never leaving her side.

❦

Machiko woke up to darkness, gasping for air, feeling her lungs burn as if she had been drowning. The dream had become more real, more vivid than usual and the suffocation sensation never seemed to subside, only grew stronger. How long had she been in hiding in her room? One? Maybe two? She couldn't remember what day it was anymore and she really didn't give a damn.

She could barely recall the events that occurred after the art show but she remembered the feeling of liberation, as if everything made sense to her at last. No, she didn't regret destroying her paintings. She believed she had reacted for the right reasons, but her actions may have thrown fresh fuel to the gossip fire. Perhaps even giving reporters ammunition to dig up her past with enough dirt to restart the rumor mills again.

Frankly, her reputation wasn't her main concern. She was certain her antics would affect the people she cared deeply about. Her parents. Luc. *Caleb.* God, would he fear she was unstable? Had she destroyed the bond they had fought so hard to maintain all because of her pride?

He didn't deserve this. He didn't deserve more pain than he had already experienced. She had to go. She couldn't stay knowing that the accumulation of all her emotional scars ran deeper than she had believed. She was afraid that sooner or later she would destroy him if she didn't work out these demons.

But she couldn't deny the real root of the matter stemmed from a much greater fear. One she needed to face head on. Machiko had to see her mother and repair the damage she had caused. Only then could she return to Caleb a whole person again. Not a broken piece of artwork he had glued together that would eventually break off with time. He deserved so much more than what she was able to give. She hoped in time he would learn to forgive her.

Machiko forced herself to get out of bed. She made a quick sweep of the house, her heart thundering against her chest. She gathered a few personal items, including her mother's letter, and shoved them into her backpack. She wanted to leave before he discovered what she was about to do. She knew that if Caleb was there to stop her, she might not have the energy to resist.

જ

The smell of cleaning products, mixed with the stench of death, lingered in her nostrils as she walked through the brightly lit hallway of the private Seattle cancer facility. Cold air blasted through the air vents, chilling her to the bone with every step. Machiko stopped in front of the ICU, fear coating her throat, her hand barely touching the steel doors.

She took a deep breath and pressed the buzzer. *Click!* The doors automatically parted and she walked through at a snail's pace. Respiratory ventilators pumped quietly in the background and the repetitive beeping of the heart monitors made her pulse race whenever she passed a hospital bed.

How long had it been since she had seen her parents? *Too long.* She swallowed hard, panic rising as she approached the petite woman sitting at the foot of a bed. Her head bent, her body appeared fragile and Machiko's heart cried out.

Almost a decade ago she had turned her back from them and now she was ready to face them again. She swallowed down the heavy lump residing in her throat. Her palms were sweaty, her body warm with regret.

She looked over at the man on the bed. Her dear father lay in slumber, pale and listless. She bit back the tears and wanted to run to him. Wanted to make everything better for him, like he did when she scraped her knees as a child.

Sakura raised her head, her worried expression transformed into surprise.

"Hoshi." She quickly slid out of the chair, her hands clutched at her side.

Machiko felt the pressure work its way from the corner of her eyes. "Mother."

The woman smiled, a soft joyous smile. A tear trickled down her cheek and she could not hold on to the hurt. Machiko took two steps forward and threw her arms around her mother, clinging tightly.

"I'm so sorry. Please forgive me," she sobbed against Sakura's shoulder.

Her mother pulled away to take a good look at Machiko. She shook her head, cupping her cheeks in her palms. "There's nothing to forgive. You're here now, that's all that matters."

✿

Caleb paced the expanse of his living room. He was beside himself when he discovered Mac had disappeared. She had packed up and left without thinking to leave a bloody letter. *Where was she?*

"There's no use working yourself over. She'll turn up and when she does she'll need a friend." Frankie handed him a drink.

He downed the contents as if it was water, his throat burning all the way down.

"Nothing beats J&B to chase the demons away," she joked as she refilled his glass.

"Why didn't she tell me? I thought she trusted me."

"How do you think Luc felt? He probably thinks he

betrayed her and we know it's not his fault. Be a friend. Don't feel sorry for yourself, it's not how you play." She tapped Caleb's chest with the bottle.

He rubbed his head. Hell, he was angry, confused, hurt. "I don't know what's going on anymore. I don't know how to feel."

Frankie took his glass and handed him the bottle. "Maybe you want to think on it. When you're finished moping, go visit Luc. He might need the company."

He watched her disappear out the back door. He didn't know what to say, how to respond. He brought the bottle to his lips and chugged the alcohol. Frankie was right, he needed to step up and figure out a way to get her back. He knew her leaving was inevitable, but not this way. Not like this.

Caleb wiped his mouth and put the bottle down. He bounded out of the house to visit his friend. He tapped on the glass door and after a few seconds Luc let him in.

The man looked nothing like his usual charming self. Dark rings were visible under his eyes and he looked like he hadn't shaved in days. Caleb rubbed his own stubbles. *Get it together, man. Luc needs you right now.*

He followed Luc to the living room and the man plunked down on the sofa. The pungent odor of cigarettes hung in the air and a burning cancer stick was in the ashtray.

Caleb made himself comfortable on the coffee table to confront the man. "Okay, this is fucking nuts. Where is she?"

Luc looked at his friend through bloodshot eyes.

"You did nothing wrong."

"I pushed her too hard. I should have listened to her and allowed her more time." He wallowed.

"Snap out of it. I don't know what the hell Jordan was thinking but it all boils down to Mac's own decisions. I want to find her as badly as you do, but maybe we just have to wait it out."

"Christ, Caleb! I caused her to have a meltdown!"

Caleb groaned, unable to get through to Luc. "Her actions are the least of our problems right now. We need to focus on damage control. I don't want the world to think Mac's gone off the deep end again. I don't want her to go through a repeat of this."

Luc milled over his words and he nodded in agreement. "*Oui*. You're right. She's been through enough pain, she doesn't need any more."

He swatted Luc on the knee. "That's the spirit. Let's put our heads together and see what we can come up with."

"Caleb." Luc gave him a weak smile. "I was able to save a few of them. They're not all lost."

❦

Machiko stroked her father's hair as he slept. Her eyes were swollen from all the tears but she had been able to bond with her mother. They had made progress and she was surprised at how easy it was to talk to Sakura. Their conversation had started the healing process, but the road to recovery was still in the distance. This was a good start and she was glad she made the decision to see them.

After much resistance, her mother agreed to go home to rest. Machiko promised to stay with her father. She wanted to be there during this crucial time. She owed him that much.

Benjamin Kingston looked like a shadow of himself. In her eyes, her father had always been larger than life. He was a strong and proud man, his talents renowned. Yet, right now in this hospital bed, he appeared human. Mortal.

She pushed the loose tendrils out of her face and noticed his shallow breathing, his body frail from the illness. She could not turn away from the endless tubes and machines hooked to his body. Benjamin had come in for a case of pneumonia and what they discovered was an early stage of cancer. The doctors had detected the illness in time and his chances of healing seemed promising. Along with treating the pneumonia, with the chemotherapy treatments, he would have a greater chance of survival.

She knew there was a greater force that brought her here

and she prayed for her father's forgiveness. She regretted the lost time and swore that she would make things right again. Her father needed to beat this illness so she would have the opportunity to make good on the promise.

Benjamin stirred, his eyes fluttered open. After several seconds he focused on her face and she saw a spark of life flashing across his eyes. She removed her hand and sat up, her heart pounded as fast as a steam engine as she waited.

He mumbled something inaudible, his eyes misting over. She leaned in so he would not strain his voice. Instead, he reached for her, touching her face. She could feel the tears flowing again and knew in that moment that everything would be okay.

"I brought some coffee. Your father suggested you might want some." The nurse's voice broke through her dream.

Machiko rubbed her eyes, waking to the faint sound of Benjamin's heart. She had fallen asleep sometime during the early morning hours. Her head was still groggy from exhaustion but she accepted the drink, thanking the woman.

She straightened up in her seat, stretching to get some circulation through her body.

"Is it really you?" Her father asked hoarsely.

Her body filled with happiness at having this chance to talk to him, even under these circumstances. She gave him a tender smile and covered her hand over his.

"Yes, father. I'm here and I'll never leave you again."

He shook his head. "The past is done and gone. Let's work on the future."

Machiko didn't let go of his hand. She missed her father and as angry as she had been with herself, the emotion had melted as soon as she saw him. Nothing would repair itself magically but she had questions and she knew he would answer them when he was well enough. For now, she wanted to concentrate on making things as easy as possible for him.

She had undergone an enormous metamorphosis these past few months. Today marked the beginning of her road to enlightenment.

Chapter Sixteen

Caleb read the sentence for the third time but nothing was sinking in. Frustrated, he threw his pen across the room and shoved the papers aside. His patience was wearing thin these days and he couldn't stop thinking about *her*.

A little over two months had passed and he hadn't even heard a peep. His private investigator hadn't been able to locate her after she pulled the vanishing act. Ironic, it mirrored the one reaction she had executed when she was thirteen. The whole damn thing puzzled him. Yet this time, she had managed to run off with his heart.

He needed to get out of here. The office, with its contemporary furnishings and incredible Santa Monica view, no longer appealed to him. Everything felt bleak and hollow, suffocating, now that Mac was gone.

Jordan had effectively ruined any progress Mac had made during these few months. His lips curled in disgust thinking about *that* night. Caleb stood up and grabbed his jacket, letting out a bitter sigh.

He missed surfing. The ocean waves had called to him for weeks but he didn't have the heart to go. The summer had faded quickly and now he was already preparing for the winter. The only thing he couldn't bear changing was his decision to keep his head clean shaven. This was a reminder that Mac was still alive and well in the confines of his heart.

His office door swung open and he glanced up. The last person he wanted to see was standing in the doorframe.

"Caleb. We need to talk." Jordan's voice was rigid, icy.

"There's nothing to discuss. Consider yourself lucky that your father transferred you back to the London office."

He continued to gather his belongings as if she wasn't there. He hadn't noticed her walk over to him, hadn't expected her to lay a hand on his forearm.

Caleb looked her in the eyes and spoke with deadly calm, "Don't *ever* touch me again."

She released his arm as if she had been burned; her expression pained. "I've already apologized. What more do you want me to do? Beg? I will, if you would only hear me out."

"Jordan, what could you possibly say that would make me change my mind about you? Forgive you?"

"I loved you. I loved you so much that my emotions blinded me. I couldn't tell jealousy from reason." Her eyes misted up. "When I realized Machiko had given you that painting, and the way you reacted, I knew it was finally over between us. I didn't want to believe the truth. Nothing went as I had planned at the art show and my desperate attempts backfired on me."

Her eyes dropped to the carpet. She continued in a tormented voice, "I wanted to hurt you. Can you fault me? I loved you all these years, ever since childhood and now there's no hope for us."

He shoved his hands in his pockets and leaned back against the edge of his desk. His heart was torn between telling her to leave and giving her time to heal her own wounds.

The tension hung in the air, but he needed time. Time to think things through without anger hanging over them. He let out a shallow breath. "I don't want to hate you. I'm fuckin' pissed as hell right now and it will take a long time before I can look at you without being angry. I won't make any promises but I think the distance will be good for both of us."

Caleb was furious with her, but he knew she hadn't meant to be cruel. They were two different people and no matter what happened, he was still her father's business partner. He couldn't let his personal feelings interfere with business.

Jordan was a shrewd businesswoman and very skilled at what she did. He also couldn't discount the fact that they had always been friends. They had known each other since they were in diapers and he didn't want to see the complete demise of their relationship.

Someday he would be able to forgive her, but his emotions were too raw right now. He needed time and hoped her returning to London would repair their friendship.

"I know I hurt you. I can't turn back time but I want you to know that as long as it takes, I will make things right," she said with sincerity.

He looked at her, his face expressionless. "Goodbye, Jordan."

She nodded in understanding and reached into her purse. She pulled out a small scrap of paper and handed it to him. "Regardless of what you think, I want you to be happy. I just wish it had been with me."

She laid it in his palm and closed his fingers over it, pausing for a brief moment before she walked out of his life.

Caleb looked down at the crumpled scrap in his hand and unfolded the paper slowly. Pain seared his heart at seeing the information inside. His brain jumped to a dozen conclusions and all of them were unsettling. He looked down at the handwriting again and prayed he had misread the message. *Dear, God! It can't be.*

It was the phone number to a private cancer facility in Seattle. His heart tore apart at the thought of Mac suffering alone.

৩১৩

"Are you sure about this?" Gemma looked like she was going to burst into tears at the drop of a hat. "I'm such an idiot. No wonder she had been acting so strangely. She was hiding the pain and we were too stupid to see the signs."

His response came out choked, "You saw it for yourself."

"Let's not jump to conclusions without getting the facts."

"You're right. I've already booked a flight out tonight. I'm going to get to the bottom of this. I'm going to make damn sure Mac will be taken care of." His tone was firm.

"Whatever you do, don't upset her."

"Gems, you know me better than that."

"And *that's* why I'm telling you to give her time to heal."

His sister's sad frown made the knot tighten in his stomach.

"You're right. I won't press things. I just need to see her. If she needs time, I'll give it to her."

Gemma hugged her arms around herself and leaned into her brother. "I really like her, Caleb."

"So do I, sis."

"I hope she keeps you," she sighed.

"Me, too."

Caleb had never wanted anything more in his life and he couldn't see his future without Mac. His mouth twisted into a sardonic smile. While he had wanted to bring out the woman in her, Mac had slowly made him become the man his father would have been proud of.

After his sister left he quickly packed and headed for the airport. As he sat on the airplane staring out the window at endless miles of darkness, he was consumed by the possibility that Mac could reject him. The sharp pain was like a twist of a dagger through his heart.

He had gotten over the feeling of betrayal when she had left without a goodbye. He had even gotten over the fact that she did not call him to let him know she was okay. But her sudden inability to trust him hurt like hell. *Why didn't she tell me the truth?*

The dull ache spread through every pore, every nerve ending in his body. Inwardly, his soul cried for her. These days, all he could think about was *her*. Machiko. The woman who had turned his world upside down the first time he laid eyes on her.

Caleb closed his eyes and leaned back against his seat. He

tried to push her image from his mind but he knew the effort was futile. He felt the sting behind his eyes and realized the last time he had shed tears for anyone was when he had buried his father.

Why did it hurt so much to think about her?

His eyes flew open as the truth simmered inside his heart. He had known all along.

He loved Machiko.

જા≋

The frosty air felt good against her face. She had been at the cancer recovery center for weeks now, sitting with her father every day. In his company she found the peace she had always longed to know. The time spent with her family had given her a new outlook. Her father had recovered from the pneumonia but he had another week of physical therapy and chemotherapy before they could discharge him.

This part of her life was balancing out; but there was another part she wasn't ready to revisit yet. She knew she needed to face the world again and show them she wasn't mentally unstable. Far from it.

In those moments when she had taken a knife to her paintings she had unleashed the person she had always been. She was stronger for it and she would face the firing squad without any regrets. She would worry about that later, when she was certain her father was well enough.

Machiko pulled her beanie over her ears and continued reading the latest paperback, an erotic novel, *Forbidden Fruit* by Eden Bradley. She was so engrossed in the delicious story she hadn't paid attention to the person taking a seat beside her on the bench.

"I don't suppose it's something I'd enjoy reading, do you?"

Her hands trembled inside the gloves. His voice was like an angel's song and she could feel the heat encompassing her heart. She didn't want to look, didn't dare. Machiko closed the book and laid it aside.

"How did you find me, Caleb?"

She shifted in her seat to look at him and a flood of excitement rushed through her.

He was so handsome in a dark wool coat and stonewashed jeans, a fitted beanie covering his head. His hands were hidden in his coat pockets and she wondered if he ached to touch her as she did for him. Her body tingled as she remembered those nights in his bed, when her favorite thing was his gentle caresses across her body, his lips and mouth taking her to new heights of ecstasy.

"Why didn't you tell me?"

"I wasn't ready to." She rubbed her hands together, suddenly affected by the cold.

His ungloved hands shot out to take her hands between his, rubbing against them to give her additional warmth. He expelled a heavy breath and stopped to stare at her.

Caleb brought her hand to his face, turning his head to kiss her palm. "I've missed you, Mac."

Her lips quivered and she yearned to tell him all the things swirling inside. She was happy to see him, longed for his kisses, craved his lovemaking, but she knew the timing wasn't right. Not now. There were still things she had to sort through and he would only be a distraction.

"I can't do this. I need to focus on myself. I need to get well. I've spent too many years running and not enough trying to fix the problems. It's time I do this and I need to do this alone." She got up hastily and picked up her book, couldn't look him in the eye.

"I've enjoyed the time with you and from the beginning you knew I would be leaving. I just need you to accept it." She couldn't look at him without wanting to cry and she turned away to return to the facility.

She didn't hear his footsteps, didn't realize he was following behind until he grabbed her arm and swung her hard against him. Her body was crushed against his solid form and he ground his mouth on hers, drawing every ounce of breath from her.

His kisses were full of anger and passion. The intensity jarred her conscience and a flurry of rapture twisted and twirled around her, erasing everything but Caleb.

His mouth was hot and hungry. His tongue lavished her mouth with thorough attention until she was intoxicated by a desire to be fulfilled. She slipped her arms around his heck, pulling him closer.

Machiko's conscience screamed its objections. She had to do the right thing or else she would have another wound to patch up. She knew full well Caleb was her weakness. She didn't have a choice; she needed to do this for his sake and keep him out of the mess she created. She had to make this right on her own.

She didn't care about her reputation anymore, but she wasn't about to see him go down with her. She had destroyed her own family and wasn't about to destroy him as well. He meant too much to her to hurt him that way.

Machiko pushed him at arm's length. "I won't let you do this to me. I don't need you hanging around like some jealous lover. It was never going to be anything other than physical. Go away and leave me alone. Just go away!"

"You don't mean that." He reached for her hand and she snatched it away.

"You were nothing more to me than a temporary distraction."

He dropped his hands and his spirit appeared to have sunk lower into anguish. "I don't know what's going on with you, but please, don't shut me out. I need you." His voice rose as if in a last effort to hold onto her. "I love you, Machiko."

Her mouth opened in dismay. She could feel her throat closing up, her body turning icy cold. He was saying everything she had wanted to hear yet she refused to believe it. The pain seared her heart.

I don't deserve your love! She wallowed in an agonizing maelstrom of sorrow; the misery became a steel weight on her soul. She had to act fast; she needed to say the words before she lost the nerve altogether.

When she finally spoke, her tone was sad, confused. "I'm

sorry. I don't know…I thought maybe…" She let out a frustrated breath, "Maybe someday there will be a possibility of us. But for now, there can't be an *us*."

His eyes darkened with pain, his expression was like someone who had been struck in the face, and an acute sense of loss knotted in her belly. *Please, forgive me.*

A sensation of intense sickness and desolation swept over her in knowing that she would live the rest of her life without him, without his touch, without his lovemaking.

She shuddered inwardly and hoped that one day he would see that she had done this all for him.

Chapter Seventeen

*T*he enormous blank wall stared back at her, ripe for the painting. Machiko stepped back, hands in the back pockets of her cutoff jeans, trying to figure out a theme for the mural. Visions of a magical forest complete with wood nymphs, elves, and sprites sprang to mind, conjuring up a dozen scenarios for her to choose from. *Yes, that's exactly what the children would love.*

This was her latest commissioned work and it brought her back to Manhattan Beach. She'd avoided the city for the past eighteen months, but fate always had a way of bringing her back to face her fears head-on. This time, she was ready for anything. Anyone.

Well, almost anyone. Machiko couldn't allow herself to think about *him* right now. She had nine weeks to finish this project before heading back to New York to present her next venture to the Board.

What started out as a philanthropic endeavor to help restore dilapidated churches, landmarks, and schools had turned into a satisfying mission that had taken her across the globe. She had developed a reputation for her murals, and now took on the occasional commissioned project to help raise funds. Even when she wasn't doing the work herself, she coordinated many of the larger international projects.

Over the past ten months, she built her small nonprofit from a struggling, high risk venture to an international success. Her program helped hundreds of underprivileged children around the world. The young muralists received scholarships while building their portfolios. At the end of the program these artists were guaranteed job placement for their commitment.

Machiko cracked her knuckles. *Time to get serious*. She had prepped the walls with a small crew the day before. They spent hours cleaning and priming the surface so she could work on the preliminaries today. Her assistant Olivia would stop by after lunch to photograph and document the project for the investors.

Her flip flops made loud flapping sounds across the concrete as she walked over to her box of art supplies. She opened it and reached inside, pausing for a moment when she felt the wrinkled newsprint. She unfolded it and there he was, shaking hands and posing with a member of the city council.

The headline read *Businessman's endowment funds local art program*. With her finger, she traced his strong jaw, tried to imagine his toffee-colored eyes in the black and white photograph.

She replaced the article and reached into the metal toolbox for the pouch of pastel chalks. She always liked to create a rough outline beforehand to use as a guide for the painting. She would most likely get through a third of the outlining today, and then continue over a three-day period.

Machiko could feel the mid-morning heat as the sun beat hard against her neck and back through the flimsy white tank top. She knew she would have a nice sunburn by the end of the day. With all the traveling she'd done over the past ten months, she'd acquired a deep tan, and the Los Angeles summer would certainly help maintain her coloring.

A gentle breeze brushed passed her and she smelled the salty ocean air, reminding her of her summer in Manhattan Beach. She felt a twinge of sadness as the memories floated through her mind. So much had changed and she no longer resembled the naïve girl she used to be. Machiko was a different person now; she'd become a woman with a mission and a purpose.

She opened the pouch, choosing a sky blue chalk to begin the initial sketch of the foliage and mythical creatures. Once she started, she became entranced in her creation and the rest of the world melted around her.

Caleb watched her from a short distance. His breath caught in his throat. *Could it be her?* He stood dumbfounded, his palms growing sweaty like a school boy observing his first crush. Mac's hair was swept high atop her head in a messy ponytail bun and her skin was now a perfect shade of brown.

His eyes skimmed the nape of her neck, the wisps of loose tendrils, and his heart hammered hard against his chest at discovering the latest adornment to her body. She sported a new Sanskrit Om tattoo at the small of her neck just below her hairline. The dark ink glistened from her moist skin and he longed to run his tongue across the image.

Caleb ran his hand over his head, still surprised to feel his own hair. He stopped shaving his head a couple of months after she sent him away. To try to force himself to move on, once he accepted that she wasn't coming back.

God, she was gorgeous! Even now, after all this time, she stirred lustful cravings inside of him. His eyes slid leisurely down her body to the delicate lotus blossom tattoo prominently displayed on her left ankle. There was no mistake: it was her.

He walked over as if in a dream state. He stood behind her, admiring the way her body stretched and moved while she sketched. His cock jolted in reaction, swelling tight against his jeans. Shit. This wasn't the time for him to become aroused. He thought he would be unaffected by her but she proved to have a stronger impact on him than he would like.

He dreaded the reunion and was ready to rush through the small talk, and then get the hell out of there before she had a chance to rip out his heart again.

What the hell was he thinking? Caleb regretted volunteering for this meet-and-greet. If he had known it was Mac he never would have agreed to go. The irony of the situation was laughable. Never in his wildest dreams would he have believed that the nonprofit company she worked for was funded by the business he'd recently acquired.

It was now or never. He took a deep breath and his voice came out deeper than he wanted. "You must be the artist we commissioned on this project."

Mac dropped the piece of chalk and it broke into several small pieces. In her crouched position, his mind drifted back to a time when he had watched her work on her paintings. He loved how graceful she was when she created. Loved the interesting techniques and positioning of her body in order to receive the exact results she wanted. She mesmerized him with her talents and in studying her now, he could easily get lost in her.

How the hell was he going to survive this visit?

She managed to stand up, pivoting around to face him. Her expression was impassive, yet cool. "Hello, Caleb."

Her voice was like an angel's song, a sweet caress to his soul. He cleared his throat, his pulse racing from her nearness. "Welcome back."

Everything he had wanted to say flew out the window as soon as she opened her mouth. He had to fight the urge to hold her in his arms. To demand why she had ended things the way she did. He wanted to be angry but his heart had another motive.

They stood staring at each other in awkward silence. He started to fidget, his fingers itching to touch her. She licked her lips and the unconscious action sent waves of impure thoughts rushing through him.

He had to restrain himself before he slammed her back against the wall and took her there in the courtyard. To punish her for depriving them both of all the pleasures they could have shared. He wanted to be cruel, to hurt her as much as she had hurt him, but he couldn't. No matter what happened between them, he still cared about her.

Snap out of it, Holden! You hate her, remember?

Yes, he recalled those cruel words she hurled at him the day she broke his heart, left him to bleed without any chance of his wounds healing. Left him to wonder if she had wasted away from illness, alone, without him by her side. The thought ate him up.

Her tone was gentle, her eyes softening. "I'll understand if you don't want to work with me. I can reschedule the meeting with Alfred if you'd like."

He shook his head. "No, it's okay. This isn't about us, Mac. It's business. Unless you're uncomfortable and would rather I go."

"You're right. This is business. It won't take more than fifteen minutes, anyway. I'll just go over the stage one concept and can send you the first phase photos in the morning."

Instantly, her demeanor changed from nervous to confident as she described her idea. She sounded professional, and her project was well thought out, yet he couldn't focus on anything she was saying.

He could see her lips moving. Those same lush lips that had wrapped around his cock and worked him up so many times before. He needed a cold splash of water or else he was going to come just thinking about all the ways he wanted to make love to her.

While he listened to her, Caleb realized she had changed not only physically but internally. As if her experiences had broken her spirit down, then built her back up again, aging her soul.

The revelation suddenly intrigued him. He wanted to learn more about the person she had become. Learn about everything that had ensued since she dismissed him that winter day at the recovery center in Seattle.

"Have dinner with me." He blurted. Jeez, he couldn't believe he had interrupted her in mid-sentence and now made things "personal".

"What?" Mac gave him a peculiar look as if she was trying to figure him out.

"I want you to have dinner with me. Tonight."

He had expected her to refuse, or better yet, make up excuses and decline. Instead, her lips curved into a seductive smile.

"I would love to."

"What?" He had been completely taken off guard. Her response made him break out in a cold sweat.

Her silky laughter penetrated his nerves. "I said, I would love to have dinner with you."

Caleb's cell phone vibrated just as he was about to respond. "I'm sorry, I have to check this."

He pulled the phone out of his pocket and reviewed the text message. "Small emergency. Looks like I need to head back to the office. Is that all right?"

"Sure. That's fine. Everything I said will be written in the report you'll receive, anyway."

"Sounds good. Um, I'll pick you up tonight at the Fairmont around eight?"

She grinned and gave him her cell number. He quickly added the information to his contacts and shoved the phone back in his pocket.

"I'll see you tonight, then." He hesitated for a moment, then extended his hand.

She looked at his hand and the briefest shadow crossed her face. She raised her eyes to his and smiled, taking his hand. "I look forward to it."

He held on a bit longer than he should. A surge of electricity spiked through his fingers, up his arm and through his system. All the dormant emotions that he managed to stow away were now unlocked and causing havoc in his subconscious.

Caleb groaned inwardly at the knowledge that when Mac breezed out of town again, she would not leave his soul unscathed. Hell, if he was a smart man, he'd hand her what's left of his heart on a silver platter and be done with it.

◦◦◦

"You're sure he's gone?" Machiko's eyes darted back and forth through the window blinds.

"Of course, dear. I would hate for him to find out I've known where you were all along and didn't tell him." Frankie's musical voice answered over her shoulders.

She heaved a sigh and turned away from the window. "I'm sorry I put you in such a terrible position. I just needed time."

Frankie reached out and squeezed her hand. "I wouldn't think of coveting any secrets except for you." Her smile was warm and cozy, reminding Machiko of fresh baked cookies.

"Thank you for everything. I owe you so much."

"Nonsense. If anyone should know what you're up to, it should be me." Frankie said in a tearful tone, "I'm so happy to see you again."

Machiko gave her a stern look. "No tears. Remember our pact?"

The older woman nodded, wiping at her eyes. "Shouldn't you be getting ready for the big date?"

"It's not really a date. I'm sure he wants to make me feel nice and secure before he pulls out the voodoo doll. Besides, the hotel's just around the corner."

"You'll be lucky if that's all he pulls out." Frankie winked.

"I have to admit I hadn't expected to see him so soon. What are the odds?" She let out a nervous laugh before continuing, "He looked good. Really good. Thanks for being there for him. It means a lot to me."

"I won't lie, he was hit pretty hard and I'm glad he pulled himself out of it."

Machiko crossed her arms. "I can't thank you enough. There were so many times I wanted to make things right but I was just so screwed up inside."

"You don't have to say anymore, Mac. It's water under the bridge and tonight you've got a shot at a new beginning. *That is*, if you want it."

She let Frankie's words swirl, weighing them against her feelings. Machiko took a deep breath. "I do want it. I want Caleb."

"Glad you finally figured it out. Well, I don't know about you, but I need a stiff drink." Frankie walked over to the mini-bar and grabbed the first bottle she spotted. She poured hefty portions of vodka into two tall glasses and handed one to

Machiko.

Machiko eyed the drink. "I suppose you're numbing me up for the first round."

"Trust me, you'll thank me later."

In spite of herself, Machiko had to laugh at her friend's ability to heighten the anticipation.

❦

The alcohol hit Machiko hard as soon as she stepped out of the taxi. She barely made it into her hotel room when she realized how late she was running. She took a quick shower then stumbled to the closet.

Her long, wet locks clung to her back, a towel wrapped around her. She glanced at the clock: a quarter to eight. *Shit. Shit. Shit!* She wasn't even remotely presentable. She slid open the double doors of the closet and a wave of melancholy hit her. How was she going to make everything right after all she had done?

Her head pounded inside her skull. She rubbed her temple, the vodka still lingering in her system. She looked past the rows of colors and her mind drifted, her body unsteady. How could she be so irresponsible? There was nothing she could do about it now.

She narrowed her selection down just as she heard a firm knock on the door. Machiko smoothed her moist hair away from her face and padded across the room to answer.

Caleb's smile died on his lips, his eyes dark and unfathomable.

"I'm a bit behind schedule." She stepped back and felt suddenly lightheaded. She swayed, trying to gain balance when her head spun out of control.

Caleb was there holding her, sweeping her into his arms. He kicked the door shut and carried her to the sofa inside the suite. Instead of laying her down on the sofa, he dropped onto the cushion and cradled her against him. She didn't protest and leaned her head closer as she listened to the rapid beating of his heart.

"You don't have to do this." Even to her, her words made her sound weak. Vulnerable.

She heard him exhale deeply. "Let's just pretend for one moment that everything is okay." His rich timbre reverberated through her and she nodded gently.

Machiko tried to resist the sorrowful emotion, but in his arms she longed for things she'd thought could never be. She had lost his trust and she wasn't sure she would ever regain it. She fought with everything in her not to cry but a hot tear rolled down her cheek, soon more tears followed.

His hand grazed her cheek, his fingers meeting with the hot liquid. She moved her head for a better view of his handsome face and he brought the moist fingers to his mouth. He tasted her tears, as though they would help him share her pain. Help him understand. She shivered as a profound ache ruptured, spilling all the anguish out to relive again and again.

He stroked her hair, wanting her to get all the tears out of her system. Deep sobs racked her body and soaked his shirt. The harder she cried the more he could feel her sorrow, could feel his own heartbreak in the process.

He settled back, holding her tight against him. He should be angry for what she had put him through, yet he couldn't bear the thought of her suffering. As he continued to console her, he secretly enjoyed their closeness, almost believed their connection had never quite abandoned them.

Gradually the hot tears slowed, reminding him of a quiet drizzle that soon trickled into silence.

Caleb woke to a kink in his neck. He was momentarily disoriented until he brushed across the soft flesh. He looked down at Mac with groggy eyes, blinking to focus on her lovely face. He watched her breasts rise and fall as she slept, could hear the gentle sound of her breathing.

How could he turn away from this? He ran his knuckles across her cheek, her lips. She shivered at his touch and settled back to sleep. He checked his watch and it was three in the morning. How the hell did that happen? He should leave but he didn't want to disturb her sleep if she needed it. Hell, he'd thought about her for a year and a half. If this was as close as she'd let him get, he'd take it.

With Mac, it wasn't all about sex. They had phenomenal physical attraction, yet there was more. Even if he could never hold her again he wanted to remember this. He inhaled the familiar scent of cherry blossoms in bloom and his lower half roused to attention, growing rigid.

He shifted, trying to find a more comfortable position and Mac snuggled closer to him. She buried her face deeper into his neck, her lips touching his skin, her breasts crushed against his chest. He would give anything to taste her again, every mouth-watering inch.

As if she could feel his torment, her lips moved, scraping across his flesh and his jaw tightened. She moved, propped up on her knees in a straddle position. Her hands peeled the towel open and the thick fabric slid around her thighs.

Caleb swallowed hard, his eyes immediately traveling over her beauty. The bulging pressure against his slacks cut into his circulation, causing a brief numbing sensation to his cock.

"Touch me, Caleb," she purred.

He blinked, his hands fisted against the cushions. "Don't do this." *Don't make it harder than it already is.*

"You're right. I don't know what I was thinking." Embarrassment stained her cheeks and she reached for her towel.

He covered her hands to stop her. His eyes caressed her soft curves, making love to her in his mind.

"You're so fucking beautiful," he exhaled.

He needed her. Needed to touch her, to feel the softness of a woman. He hadn't had the urge to be with anyone else since she left him. He devoted himself to work and had little time to look or think of another woman.

Caleb sat up, buried his hands into her thick hair and pulled her closer. He looked into her eyes, staring into the liquid depths before capturing her lips. He kissed her savagely, angrily, desperate to make her understand how much she had destroyed him. His brutal kisses left her mouth bruised, but he didn't give a damn.

She didn't fight him, her hands molding and gripping his shoulders, clawing into his skin. From the outside her behavior may have changed but inside, her passion had never waned, still burned on like a raging fire. Mac melted in his mouth, tasted like rich caramel, sweet and creamy, so light that he couldn't control his need to take what he could.

She pulled back from him. "Caleb. We need to talk."

He shook his head. "Not now. You started this and I'm going to finish it."

Chapter Eighteen

Caleb bent her back against the cushions, his body leaning into her as he parted her thighs with his hips. Mac dripped with desire and longed for the skin-to-skin contact she had missed so much. Some nights were unbearable, knowing he was out there and she wasn't with him. She often cried herself to sleep and believed she would someday be with him again, like this.

Her mind swirled with memories as she unbuttoned his shirt. She ran her hands across his chest, recalling those days when he had been the one doing the seducing.

Caleb shook a finger at her, a devilish twinkle in his eyes. His body partially covered hers and he traced his fingertip across her lip, sliding down her throat, searing a path down her abdomen to her thighs. His touch was light as he explored her inner thighs before moving back up to settle on her hips.

She arched her back as thrills of delight sparked across her skin. He cupped her breast, gently massaging, sending currents of lust flowing through her. His tongue flicked across a puckered nipple, moving to the other, tantalizing the buds which had swollen to their fullest.

"I want you to show me what you like." His voice was thick, his eyelids heavy. He reached for her hand and placed it over her breast, encouraging her to explore her own body.

She wanted to please him and slowly cupped her breasts, massaging, squeezing them. Her eyes stayed on his and she could see the arousal blazing as he watched. She caught her hardened nipples between her fingers and rolled them back and forth, pinching, pulling hard. Moisture gathered between her legs and a moan escaped her lips.

Caleb took in a quick breath. She'd already seized the advantage. Her hand slid down ever-so-slowly, skimming across her ribcage, moving lower until she reached her sex. He watched in fascination as she dipped her fingers between the slick, soft folds.

She pushed inside and the warm, moist heat coated her fingers as she moved them in and out, flicking a thumb over her clit to enhance the sensation. She raised her hips, enjoying what her hand was doing while imagining it was him.

"That's it baby, come for me," he urged seductively. His hand stroked her belly while he focused on her face, her reaction.

She bit her bottom lip, her fingers wet and soaking from desire. She squirmed as the tension mounted, her fingers tweaked and pulled at the sensitive flesh, sliding in and out. Pumping fast and hard. She felt the first tremors of arousal, the sensation spread like a blistering fire across her body.

"God, I'm coming," she cried. Her body shuddered, her hips bucked from the intensity of her release. She slowly came down from the explosion, drowning in a flood of pleasure, lost in the liberation of her mind and body.

"You are so fucking hot," he ground out.

Caleb slid down her body, pushing her thighs apart before his mouth covered her. He drank her sweetness, lapping the juices from her recent surrender. His tongue explored the pink nub of her clit, sucking softly. She wriggled beneath him but his mouth held her captive, his hands gripping her bottom as he deliberately prolonged her pleasure.

Heat rippled under her skin. Her body hummed with lust as he continued savoring her, his tongue never letting up as he drove inside. He fucked her pussy with his tongue, imagining it was his cock driving into her.

Electricity, generated by the sweet turbulence of her passion, swirled around until she couldn't hold on anymore. Her body tensed, her sanity dissipated, and she convulsed as another orgasm ripped through her, carrying her off into a world that only belonged to the two of them. Sacred. Untouchable.

⚜

Machiko stared up at the miniature chandelier attached to the vaulted ceiling. She shivered and hugged the chenille blanket tighter. She didn't know what to think of his visit tonight. Caleb had given her the best orgasm she had ever experienced and then left her in a mad rush. She gnashed her teeth, her body unfulfilled and craving him desperately.

Her mouth tingled from his kisses and she brought a finger to her swollen lips. She had hoped he would stay but didn't dare beg him to. Machiko hadn't slept a wink and her body was completely exhausted. She hoped she would have the energy to concentrate on work in a few hours.

Damn Caleb! His actions tonight proved he wasn't going to make it easy on her. What better way to torture her than to make her crazy with lust for him and then walk away?

Machiko kicked off the blanket. She had been through enough. She had fought—and won—too many battles over the past eighteen months to retreat when it came to this man. She had never wanted to be with anyone more in her life. Right then, she decided that she was going to fight fire with fire.

She arrived at work dragging her ass. The sketching had distracted her briefly, yet she was impatient to get home and had a hell of a time getting all the tree branches to look just right. Her muscles ached from the constant stretching and bending.

She didn't hear Gemma approach until her pleasant voice broke her train of thought. "A little birdie told me you're back in town."

She whirled around and squealed, "Gemma!" The women embraced as if time hadn't come between them. As if Mac's friend understood the reason she abandoned her.

Gemma held her at arm's length to get a good look. "God, I'm jealous. You look amazing!"

"So do you. I can't believe you're here." Elation swept through Machiko and she grinned.

"I figured I'd drop by to welcome you back. It's after five, and I thought you'd like to get a beer. Maybe some dinner."

"Sounds perfect. Let me put up my stuff and we'll go." She gathered up the loose items.

Gemma helped her with the task. When they finished putting away the last of the materials, she gave Machiko a caring look. "You've never looked better. Are you recovering okay?" She covered her mouth, "Oh God. I didn't mean to be so blunt about it."

Machiko's brows drew together. She stood up to meet Gemma's gaze. "I'm fine. I'm recovering very well."

"That's good. I didn't want you to go it alone, without someone there for you."

"Well, I had my parents. Even went back to therapy to straighten up a few things. As you can tell, I'm feeling a lot better." Machiko shut the art box, her eyes grazing across the picture of Caleb before she shut and locked the container.

As they walked across the street to a cozy English pub, they talked about Gemma's shoe line and her success. When the appetizers came, Machiko popped a french fry into her mouth. She missed these outings with Gemma, and although she now had many people to hang out with, it wasn't the same. No one could replace her friend's directness and sense of humor. In some ways, they were a lot alike.

"How long are you here for?" Gemma brought the beer to her lips and took a swallow.

"Nine weeks, then I go wherever my new project takes me."

Gemma's expression grew serious, thoughtful. "Was it difficult? I mean, being away from Caleb and dealing with such a terrible illness all alone."

Machiko almost choked on her beer. She wiped the back of her hand across her mouth and set the drink down. "If you mean when I went berserk and slashed through my paintings at the art show, then yes, it was difficult. And I got through it. But I'm not sure it qualifies as an illness."

Gemma blew a lock of curls off her face. She scooted closer, whispering. "Not *that*. I don't mean to pry, but—I'm talking about the *other* illness." She squeezed Machiko's hand in sisterly concern.

"Just for the record, I don't have any mental illness. Not exactly." Machiko didn't know what the hell her friend was talking about. She assumed the woman was worried about her meltdown but that was done and over with.

Gemma's eyes grew misty. "If you don't want to talk about it, it's fine. I won't press you. I just want to make sure you're alright."

"I don't have a clue what you're talking about. I'm starting to think there's something wrong with me that I don't know about."

Gemma took a deep breath and whispered, "The cancer."

"Cancer? Who has cancer?"

Gemma said in exasperation, "You! The reason you went to Seattle to get treated."

"What?" Machiko lowered her voice to a whisper, "No. No. No. I don't have cancer. My father does. Did. He's in remission now. And why are we whispering?"

Her friend teared up and threw her arms around Machiko's shoulders, hugging her tight. She finally let go and her voice rose happily. "I'm so glad to hear you don't have cancer! Not that I'm happy it's your dad and not you. Well, fuck it. You know what I mean."

"What gave you the idea that it was me?"

"Caleb discovered that you'd gone to a cancer facility. Since we didn't understand why you had left so quickly, we assumed the worst. Oh my God. I was so worried and distraught over the whole thing."

"So that's why Caleb came to see me."

Gemma nodded sadly, "He wanted to be there for you. He was devastated and I think he felt helpless. When you told him you didn't want to see him anymore, it sucked the life out of him. He flew out many times to see you, but could never follow through. I guess he thought you'd hate him if he pushed too hard."

She was grateful to hear those words. Caleb had come to see her! Wow, she was the fool. All this time she believed he had moved on without her. She buried herself in the nonprofit so she wouldn't have time to think about him. Suffering silently.

Machiko picked at the hole at the knee of her worn denims. "Why don't you hate me, Gemma? Why are you being so nice to me after what I've done? Especially to Caleb."

"Because deep down I know you love him. He might not see why you did the things you did; but you needed to do them. I can't hate you for wanting to find yourself. Hell, I wouldn't have had the balls to do half the things you did, but I hope I know you well enough to know that you wouldn't have done them without a damn good reason. I've been there before myself." She grabbed her beer as a flash of pain flitted across her eyes. "I'm not going to lie. You're gonna have to work damn hard if you want him back. You hurt him, Mac. You hurt him bad."

"I know. Looking back, I thought it was the right thing to do. How could I give love, when I was so twisted inside that I couldn't even love *myself*? I'm a different person now than I was then. Now I want Caleb. I'm ready to give him what we both deserve."

"And you'll do whatever it takes?"

"I'd walk on hot coals to win him back."

"Anything?" Machiko could see the wheels in her friend's head turning.

"Anything. Because I love him, Gemma. I always have."

She beamed, genuinely delighted with Machiko. "Well then, I'm going to help you win my brother back."

She gave Gemma a tender smile. "I'm glad you're back in my life."

Gemma blushed and rolled her eyes, "The truth is that you just want me for my shoes. Admit it."

Machiko laughed at Gemma's endearing look. "Guilty! You know me too well. Who wouldn't want a pair of Gemma Holdens?"

They both shared in the laughter and Machiko discovered how much she missed their relationship. Missed having a friend. She never believed she needed anyone before; but now, being here with Gemma, she realized what she had lost by not having friends. People she trusted, to share the trials and tribulations with.

Machiko would never be alone again.

⚜

Caleb rubbed his eyes. The contracts were starting to run together; and with the two other business ventures he had recently acquired, the work load would keep him busy for months to come.

He heard a light rap on the door and barked, "Come in."

His assistant probably had more paperwork for him. Just what he needed. He didn't bother to look up. "Just set whatever it is right on the corner of my desk."

It wasn't until he heard the splash of folders on the floor and someone making herself comfortable on his desk that he looked up.

Mac stated innocently, "If you insist."

His eyes took in the sexy, black vinyl sling-back stilettos, moved leisurely up the cinnamon colored legs, and it fully registered: this wasn't a dream. He followed the smooth, curved, vertical line until he reached the hem of her exceedingly short dress.

Caleb leaned back in his executive chair and tapped the

Montblanc pen against his knuckles, trying his best to appear unruffled by her visit. "I assume you're here because you have updates on the project." *Please let that be the reason.*

"Actually, I wanted to clear the air. I didn't get the opportunity last night." She uncrossed her legs and re-crossed them again. Giving him a not-so-subtle peek.

He shifted uncomfortably in his seat. "I don't think there's much to discuss."

Mac threw her head back and threaded a hand through her hair. He cringed. What was she up to?

"Oh, I think there's plenty to discuss." She hopped off the desk and he dropped the pen.

"What is it that you really need?" He asked in a husky tone.

She placed her hands on either side of the armrests and leaned forward. He could feel beads of perspiration forming on his brows. Mac wasn't wearing a bra and he could see the swells of her breasts and the barest hint of dark pink surrounding her perfectly taut nipples.

Her lips moved deliciously slow. "I need you." Her answer sounded way too suggestive.

He became tongue-tied. He didn't know what would kill him first: her intoxicating natural musk or her evocative body language.

"Wh—what do you need from me?" He fought for control of his brain.

Her lashes fluttered against her cheeks and her eyes pierced his. He could almost see specks of gold within their charcoal depths.

"Well, I need..." She leaned in, whispering, her lips barely touching his. "I. Need. A. Date."

"A *what*?" His eyes widened and the cloudiness in his brain evaporated.

Mac backed off and dropped her hands. She pulled a one-eighty on him and sounded as if she had never tried seducing him. "I need a date for the fundraiser dinner on Friday night. Everyone has a date except me."

He took a huge gulp of air, his body having a hard time

recovering from the heightened sexual energy that had passed between them.

"I... um..." He stumbled, unable to get the sentence out.

She squealed and clapped her hands together. "Oh, thank you. You're a lifesaver." She gave him a peck on the cheek and he felt insulted.

"Thank you for being a friend. We *are* friends, aren't we?" She batted her eyelashes and his heart stopped. This wasn't the Mac he knew. She was using her powers of sensuality to get to him.

She continued chattering, "I know it must be difficult for you and all. I hope you're okay with this?"

He nodded his head, then realized she had decided for him. He shook his head forcefully in refusal. "No, I didn't say—"

She continued as if she hadn't heard. "No need to pick me up. I'll have the car drop me off at your place. Around seven-ish?"

She blew him a quick kiss and pivoted around, swaying her hips as she walked across the room and out the door.

Caleb let out a long breath. What the hell just happened? What was going on with her? He didn't know what kind of game she was playing, but he was damn sure going to find out.

He glanced down at the bulge in his pants. Aw, hell. Now he needed to hit the gym to work out some frustration.

Machiko couldn't stop giggling as she walked down the hall. She got to her car and dialed Gemma's number on her cell phone.

"So—did it work?" Gemma asked eagerly.

"Like a charm. He didn't know what hit him," Machiko giggled.

"Men are such suckers. We work our magic, maybe wiggle our hips, and bingo!"

"I really think the magic is in the shoes. One look at your latest creation and I had him. Hook, line, and sinker."

Chapter Nineteen

She pressed the doorbell at exactly seven o'clock.

Caleb opened the door and her heart leapt in her throat. He wore a fitted tuxedo, his spiky hair perfectly styled, reminding her of a GQ cover model. Machiko's eyes automatically returned to his head. It had taken her a while to get used to his clean-shaven head, and now she had to retrain herself to appreciate his thick, dark locks.

"Aren't you punctual?" He gave her a boyish smile that made her knees weak.

"I actually came on time because I was hoping you could let me into Luc's house. There are a few things I need in there."

"I don't see why not." When he finally took a good look at her, he noticed her attire and his expression changed. "I hope I'm not overdressed. It certainly doesn't look like rain. Why are you wearing a trench coat?"

She bit back a smile. "Didn't you hear the forecast? There's a chance it could get wet tonight."

He raised a brow. "Really?"

She smiled. "A real soaker. Ready to go next door?"

Caleb grabbed the keys and they walked quietly across the

sand. Her heels sunk into the surface and she smiled, remembering their first date. He had taken her to Gemma's event. A strange tingle kissed her skin. She looked over at him and took his hand in hers.

She had expected him to pull away, but he held on as they made their way up the steps to the porch. Caleb slid the key into the lock and opened the door, allowing her to enter first.

"What I need is in the studio." She ambled ahead of him.

She could hear his footsteps echo through the house, could hear him stop and whistle from behind her. "Wow, the Delacroix must have redecorated. It's so different from what they normally like. I haven't been in here since... well, in a while."

Machiko didn't respond and rushed into the studio before he did. She stopped in the middle of the room, quickly untying the belt of her trench coat. She threw the garment in the corner and waited. She felt like she had run a marathon, and her rapid heartbeat was the result of her efforts.

A euphoric feeling filled her every pore, for tonight was the first step in "Operation Wooing Caleb", as Gemma had affectionately labeled it. She took a deep breath, exhaling to calm her jittery nerves. She was taking a huge leap of faith and knew the stakes were high. What she was risking was more than just her heart. She prayed she wasn't too late to win him back.

Caleb stepped inside the studio and was enveloped by the soft glow of candles. Coral and crimson rose petals were strewn across the floor in a path to the center of the space. Mac stole the very breath from him. She appeared like a goddess rising from a delicate pool of pink and red petals. Her white satin and tulle gown grazed her thighs, the hem floating like layers of silky clouds around her body, so transparent he could see the outline of her form beneath the material.

His eyes caught a flash of red elegantly displayed off to the side. She had constructed a bed of scarlet satin with matching pillows. Several small covered platters sat alongside a champagne bucket and pair of crystal flutes.

His curiosity flared and his eyes returned to Mac.

"I gather we aren't attending any fundraisers tonight." His mouth formed an impish smile.

"I had something else in mind." She smoothed her dress, her hands sensually moving across the curves of her body.

"Why are you doing this?" He crossed his arms to wait for her explanation. To keep the wall sturdy around his heart.

Mac traveled down the rose petal path at a leisurely pace, her hips swaying, alluring in her sensuality. She stood facing him and her smile started to melt the last of his resistance.

"I'm doing this because I love you," she said in a broken voice.

He dropped his hands and squared his shoulders back. "And you're absolutely sure?"

"I've always loved you, Caleb." Her smile brightened at a memory. "Loved you since the moment you handed me those homemade cookies. Loved you when you thought you were rescuing me from drowning. I loved you when you saved me from myself. I just didn't have the guts to tell you. *Until now.*"

His arm shot out and encircled her waist, drawing her to him, one hand on the small of her back. "God, Mac. Those were the words I've been waiting to hear. You're the only woman I've ever truly wanted. Needed. Desired."

She tilted her head, wound her arms inside his jacket and around his back. "I love you. I'm sorry it took me so long to figure it out."

"You're here now. That's all that matters to me." He crushed her mouth, claiming her with a fierce passion finally unleashed from his heart.

He kissed her with all the hunger that he'd kept locked away for so long. His tongue explored the recesses of her mouth, tasted the soft fullness of her lips, and stoked the passion of their love with every kiss.

He scooped her in his arms and carried her across the room, gently easing her down onto the makeshift satin bed. He quickly stripped off his clothes while she watched. Her eyes shimmered with the light from the window, her head cushioned by the pillow, her long locks spread out around her head and framing her face. She reminded him of an exotic mermaid, calling to him with her siren's song.

Caleb rejoined her, planting a gentle kiss on her lips. He had waited so long for this moment. The hollow in his soul was finally filling up. With every kiss, every touch, she was soothing the ache, healing the wounds. Breathing new life into him.

He undressed her slowly, his hands grazing her body as he slipped the fabric over her head. Her breasts flowed freely from their captivity, and his hands roamed intimately over the perfect swells, brushing her nipples with his thumbs. She let out a tormented groan and the heady invitation was all he needed to possess her.

His body imprisoned her as he spun a web of growing arousal, tucking her curves neatly into the contours of his own body, gorging himself on her like a man on a desert island without an ounce of water. She writhed beneath him, eager for him to touch her.

The shapely beauty of her naked form taunted him and his hands slid to cup her round bottom. A warm, thin scrap of lace was the only thing keeping their bodies from completely touching.

She threaded her hands in his hair, running her fingers gently across his skull, massaging while she returned his kisses with equal enthusiasm. He had never felt more alive! She set off sparks of pleasure with her tongue. Her sweet mouth triggered memories of the wicked things she had once done to him. He ripped away the piece of delicate lace, tearing down the only remaining barrier between them.

They were flesh against flesh now, able to take the time to explore, to arouse, to give each other pleasure. He broke away from their kiss.

"What are these?" He eyed the four covered silver platters.

"Why don't we find out?" Her naughty smile made his cock twitch.

He reached out and uncovered one lid at a time. A blindfold

with a satin scarf, a bowl of melted chocolate, a plate of strawberries and cherries, several paint brushes.

"Are you trying to seduce me?" He brushed his lips against hers.

"I was hoping." Her eyes sparkled with a smoldering fire.

He grabbed the blindfold and immediately slipped it over her head to cover her eyes. She trembled beneath him, her arousal stirred by his act. He dipped two fingers into the melted dark chocolate and touched her lips.

He slid his fingers down her chin, her throat, to the hollow between her breasts. When the trail faded, he dipped his fingers back into the chocolate and continued down her torso, her abdomen, below her belly button and stopping at the cleft between her legs.

Satisfied with the route he'd mapped, he bent his head to kiss her, his mouth and tongue following the path he had created. He reached her thighs and pushed them apart, burying his head between them, luxuriating in her softness, feasting on her sweet flesh.

She ground herself against his mouth and he continued sucking on her clit, lapping her juices, biting and teasing her until her body shivered. He brought her to the brink of orgasm and when she was close to coming he slid up her body.

He thrust hard into her, his cock slipping inside her moist warmth, and she wrapped around him like a silken glove. He groaned, pumping into her, loving the slickness. Loving how deep he was inside of her. So deep he could feel himself touch her womb. The thought of someday filling her with his seed, creating something beautiful together in this warm, safe place, made his heart soar with affection.

You're mine now, Machiko, body and soul. And I'm yours.

He pounded into her and she clawed at his back, moaning her pleasures, urging him on. They moved together, their bodies in exquisite harmony with one another. She scraped her nails across his back and dug into the flesh at his hips. He could feel the building tension, could feel their heartbeats joining in their rhythm and his control tumbled.

He pulled his stiff and throbbing cock out then rammed hard inside her. He felt her squeeze tight around him, like a satin fist, and he gasped in sweet agony, yanking off the blindfold. He needed to see her, her eyes, her face. Their bodies fit flawlessly together, bound by an indescribable force. He plunged his cock deeper still and their pleasure soared, exploding into a downpour of twinkling stars that filled their souls.

✺

Machiko watched the splash of colors, of ginger, carmine and gold, painted across the sky on an infinite canvas. She caressed Caleb's arm as he held her, their naked bodies still moist from their lovemaking.

She couldn't believe she had denied them both the pleasures of uniting the body with the heart and soul. Looking back, she realized their lovemaking had been a kind of therapy. Though she hadn't been aware of it, whenever Caleb moved inside her, he was filling a void she never knew existed. He was reconstructing the gate to her heart that allowed love and trust to slip through.

He pressed his lips against the back of her head. "I tried to visit you."

She brought his hand to her lips and tenderly kissed his palm. "I know." She rolled around to look at him.

"Remember the day at the park bench? I wanted to confront you, to see if you were battling your demons alone, to tell you that I loved you. When you turned me away, I headed back to the airport to catch a flight out." He reached out and stroked her hair. "I felt sorry for myself, even let myself go for a few days. Then I decided I needed to fight for you. I couldn't let you slip through my fingers so easily. So I called the hospital looking for you. I asked for Machiko Barrett, then Hoshi Kingston. The nurse was confused. She said that a Hoshi Kingston wasn't registered, but that a Benjamin Kingston was."

"I can't imagine how you must have felt believing I was sick." She placed her hand over his.

He ran his thumb across her lips. "When I realized you were safe, I knew you needed the time to be with your family. You needed to support your father while he was going through his battle with cancer. Don't get me wrong, I was still hurt. Devastated. For a long time, I was angry that you didn't want me to be a part of your life."

She shook her head. "I couldn't cope with it all. With my own confusion, my father's illness, what was happening between us. The truth was that I didn't think things would work out for us if I let you in. I was afraid I would drive you away with my instability. I didn't know who I was, and it ate me up inside."

"I understand now. All along I believed you didn't trust me enough to share in your pain. After all we had been through, I couldn't help feeling a little betrayed." His voice dropped.

She took his hand and placed it on her heart. "I wanted to protect you. But in doing so, only hurt you. And myself. When I think of all the lost time... I can also see that our separation changed me. I figured out who I was and what I wanted to be." She traced his jaw with her fingertips, looking into his eyes. "I never stopped thinking of you. I even saved newspaper clippings of your accomplishments. As much as it hurt me to stay away, I thought it was the best thing for both of us."

He kissed her lips and the painful knot dissipated. He shifted into a sitting position and she followed suit.

"Let's not dwell in the past. I want today to mark a new beginning for us, Mac. I'm asking you to stay with me. Don't leave."

Tears welled in her dark eyes as she looked at him through her lashes. She laid her hand across his heart. "Well, considering you're the first guest in my new home..." She smiled. "Luc drove a hard bargain, but eventually caved in." She let him register the new fact. "I thought you might want to put your house up for sale and move in with me. You've always loved this place."

She waited and when he didn't answer she continued, "I'm asking you to share your life with me. I want you to stay with me. For as long as you'll have me."

He grabbed her waist and pulled her to him. "You bet your sweet ass."

He kissed her neck and she laughed when he tickled her with his stubble. Machiko playfully pushed him away. "Hey! I was just wondering about something. If you knew I wasn't sick, then why did Gemma think I had cancer?"

He stopped kissing her and his expression grew serious. "When you left, you left both of us. Gemma really cares for you and it hit her just as hard. I guess there was an unspoken agreement between us never to bring you up. I'm sure she thought it would be too painful for me and I wouldn't be able to move forward if we continued to talk about you."

"You should have seen my face when she asked me about my illness." She waved her hand. "Well, she's all straightened out now. Everything worked out. That's all that matters."

He smacked her sharply on the butt, the sound echoing through the room. "Enough about my sister. Come over here, woman. I need you to tell me again how much you love me."

Machiko lunged for him and he fell flat on his back. She was sprawled across his body. "Actually, I'm more interested in practicing Shibari techniques on you with my scarf."

He took her by surprise and rolled her onto her back. "Not if I can help it, but I'm more than happy to practice on *you*."

The wicked gleam in his eyes made her body flush. She had something entirely different in mind. "For the rest of our lives."

Epilogue

The sun warmed Machiko's face, spreading down her body like warm honey. She gazed into the distance at the clear, blue water, and her heart swelled with happiness at how much she had grown. She had come full circle, and in understanding herself she was able to grasp the importance of love.

She adjusted her Bluetooth and listened to her father rattle off at the other end of the line.

"Yes, Dad, we got here just fine. We're both a bit jet-lagged, but Bora Bora is breathtaking. I'm actually trying to get some sun now."

She picked up the paperback propped against her stomach and put it off to the side as she listened.

"Yes, Dad," she smiled. "I put sunscreen on. I know. I love you, too. I'll be home late next week. Tell Mom I love her. What? Wait..." The phone made rustling noises and her father handed the object to her mother.

"Yes. We're having a wonderful time. Grandchildren? Don't you think it's a little too soon?" She pushed a loose tendril behind her hair.

"Okay, Mom. I'm about to head back to meet Caleb. Of course, I'll tell him you miss him. I'll call again tomorrow. Love you." She pressed the disconnect button on her Bluetooth and groaned.

Machiko loved her parents dearly, but sometimes they had a way of driving her crazy. Their latest obsession this week was grandchildren. The thought made her body tingle and she touched her flat belly. Maybe it wasn't such a bad idea after all. They would certainly have fun trying.

She grinned and lifted her face up to the sun. The brilliant rays warmed her all the way down to her toes. Ever since she bridged the gap between herself and her family, she had never felt more complete. Well, almost. Her thoughts drifted back to her husband. He always put a smile on her face and even alone on the beach, she could feel his presence. His love was as bright as the sun.

Her body suddenly ached to be with Caleb and she packed her beach items, rushing to get back to the private bungalow to make love to her husband. He'd probably ask if they had enough time, and still make their dinner reservations. She laughed. Of course there was.

She walked up the sandy path to the private garden bungalow. Bora Bora had been her dream vacation, an almost magical place. She had fallen in love with the brochures her travel agent sent her. The lagoon resembled an artist's palette of crisp, clear blues and greens.

The reality didn't disappoint. This was a romantic honeymooner's getaway with its castle-like Mount Otemau piercing the sky. The island was a photographer's wet dream with the lush tropical slopes and valleys, the blossoming hibiscus and exotic plants that decorated the palm-covered motu circle of the lagoon like a delicate necklace. To add to the picture of perfection, smooth white-sand beaches gave way to emerald waters, where a multitude of colored fish animated the coral gardens.

She arrived at their bungalow and kicked off her flip-flops at the front door. Her eyes caught sight of Caleb's surfboard propped against the wall as she entered the spacious quarters. She slid off her wrap as she padded through the room, could hear the outdoor shower running in the private tropical garden.

Machiko placed her beach bag on the dining table just as Caleb walked in from his shower. Her body instantly burned red hot at seeing his moist skin and the gorgeous dragon tattoo she loved so much. Her eyes slid lower and she licked her lips. His six-pack abs were enhanced by the nice bronze color of his skin, a result of the daily surfing back home and on the island.

Caleb rubbed his head as he dried his hair, a towel wrapped snugly around his hips. "Is everything okay, baby?"

She had heard his question but it didn't fully register in her head. All she could think about was what she would like to do to him. What she'd like him to do to her.

She continued to devour him with her eyes and he gave her a broad smile, his eyes twinkling as he continued drying his hair.

She snapped out of her momentary daydream and eyed him curiously. "Why are you smiling?"

He shrugged and she walked over to him in her black skull bikini, specks of sand still clinging to her body. This bathing suit was one of his favorites, and she'd brought it along just for him.

He pulled the towel away from his head. She gasped, then grinned, elation radiating from her surprise at his selfless action.

Caleb had shaved his head.

Her eyes glistened with tears. This was another sign of his unconditional love for her. Her heart expanded with exhilaration, recalling that summer two years ago. He had allowed her to shave his head as an ultimate sign of trust. Now, he proved that he still trusted her completely. She couldn't have asked for a better wedding present.

She wrapped her arms around his neck. He wiped her

tears and kissed her with a passion that made her temperature rise. She ran her hand across his smooth scalp and cupped his cheek.

"Yes, everything is perfect now."

Author Bio

Jax Cassidy is a multi-published author and has written under the pen name Cassidy Kent. She is Co-Founder of Romance Divas, an award winning romance writer's website and discussion forum. In between skydiving for charity and campaigning against human trafficking, she enjoys the company of close friends and indulges her caffeine fix at the nearest cafe. An avid traveler and an adventurous spirit, Jax has drawn inspiration from her experiences and often blends the exotic mix of Eastern and Western lifestyles into her writing. When she isn't locked up in her office penning her latest manuscript, Jax can be found creating abstract paintings for future art shows, or dividing her time between California, Texas, and Florida.

To learn more about Jax, visit her online at:
www.jaxcassidy.com or ww.jaxadora.blogspot.com.

Parker Publishing, LLC

Celebrating Black
Love Life Literature

Mail or fax orders to:
12523 Limonite Avenue Suite #440-438
Mira Loma, CA 91752
phone: (866) 205-7902 fax: (951) 685-8036 fax
or order from our Web site: www.parker-publishing.com

orders@parker-publishing.com

Ship to:

Name: _____

Address: _____

_____

City: _____

State: _____ Zip:_____

Phone: _____

Qty	Title	Price	Total

Shipping and handling is $3.50, Priority Mail shipping is $6.00 FREE standard shipping for orders over $30

Add S&H Alaska, Hawaii, and international orders – call for rates

CA residents add 7.75% sales tax

Payment methods: We accept Visa, MasterCard, Discovery, or money orders.
NO PERSONAL CHECKS.

Payment Method: (circle one): VISA MC DISC Money Order

Name on Card: _____

Card Number: _____ _____

ExpDate: _____

Address: _____

_____

City: _____

State: _____ Zip:_____